BLACK HISTORICAL FIGURES

MILITARY

TABLE OF CONTENTS

27
JOSEPHINE BAKER

MICHELLE HOWARD
139

115 FRANK PETERSEN

These Workbooks are geared to intrigue, inspire and motivate you to want to learn more about these Black Historical Figures(BHFs) and others. Also to do more research on your own. We know this isn't all the history of these individuals. We want you to do some of the research also. We try to be as accurate as possible during our research. If there are some stories or questions that aren't as stated, please contact us at info@wegonnalearntoday.com.

Robert Smalls

Robert Smalls

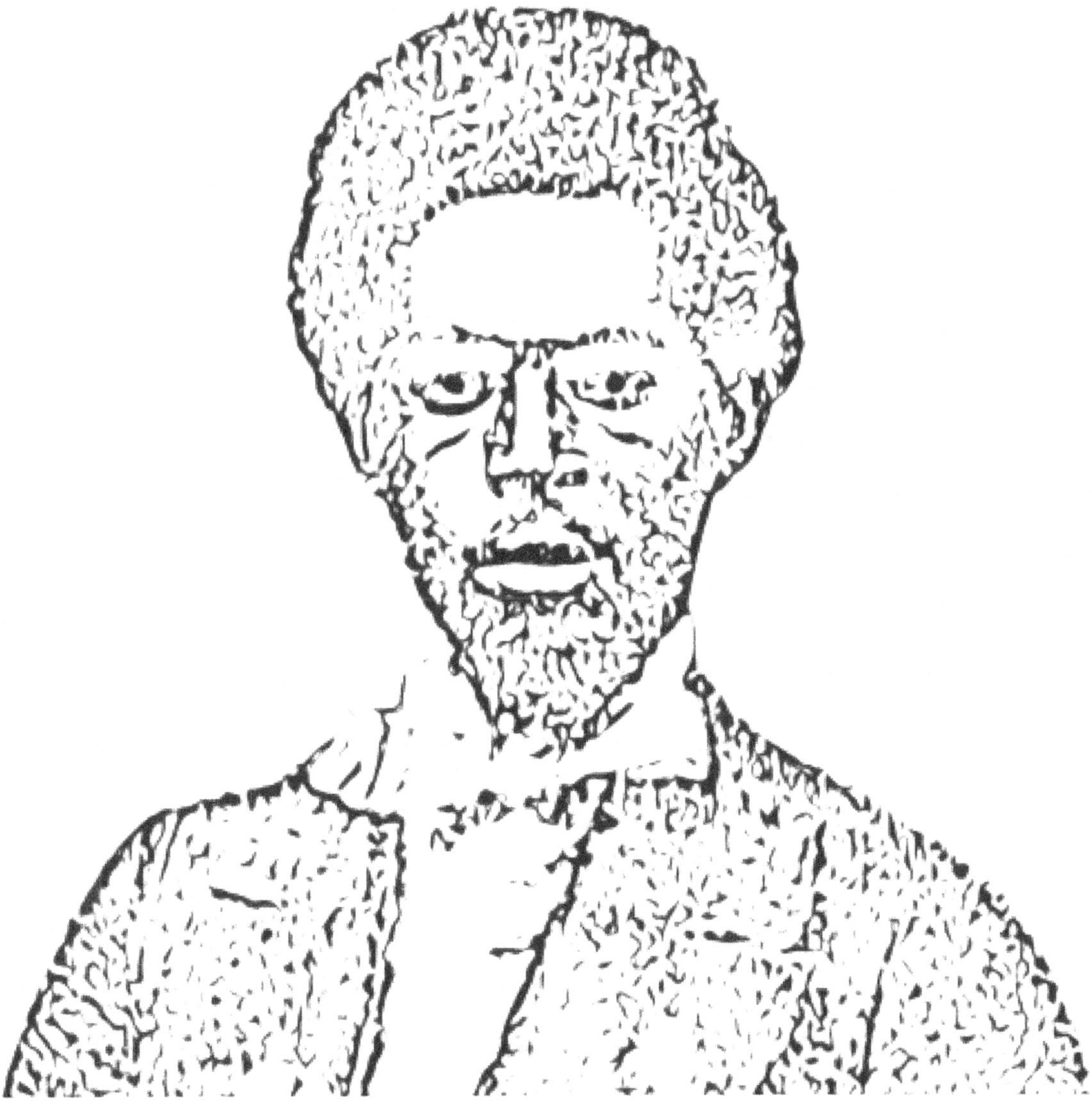

April 5, 1839 – February 23, 1915

MARITIME PILOT

3

LEFT BLANK ON PURPOSE

Robert Smalls

Robert Smalls

Robert Smalls

Robert Smalls

Robert Smalls

Robert Smalls

Directions: read the bio below and answer the following questions.

Hi, my name is Robert Smalls. I was born on April 5, 1839, in Beaufort, SC. I loved the sea and during my teenage years, I found work on the docks and wharfs. I worked as a longshoreman, a rigger and a sail maker and worked my way up to become a helmsman. I was very knowledgeable about Charleston Harbor. During the Civil War in 1861, I was assigned to steer the Confederate's CSS Planter, which was a lightly armed Confederate military transport. My duties were to survey waterways, lay mines and deliver dispatches, troops and supplies. In 1862, I was able to pilot the Planter to the Union Navy fleet. I turned over the Planter, its artillery, ammunition and the captain's code book, that contained Confederate signals and a map of the mines that had been laid in Charleston's harbor. In 1863, I was promoted to the rank of captain and was made the acting captain of the Planter. In 1864, I was made an unofficial delegate to the Republican National Convention in Baltimore.

1. Which skill didn't I learn when I was young?
   A. Rigger
   B. Sail Maker
   C. Singer
2. What war did I become a Captain in?
   A. Civil War
   B. World War I
   C. World War II
3. What was the name of the ship I was a Captain of?
   A. USS Onward
   B. CSS Planter
   C. USS Keokuk

Directions: Answer the questions, to solve the crossword puzzle. You can use the internet if you get stuck on any question.

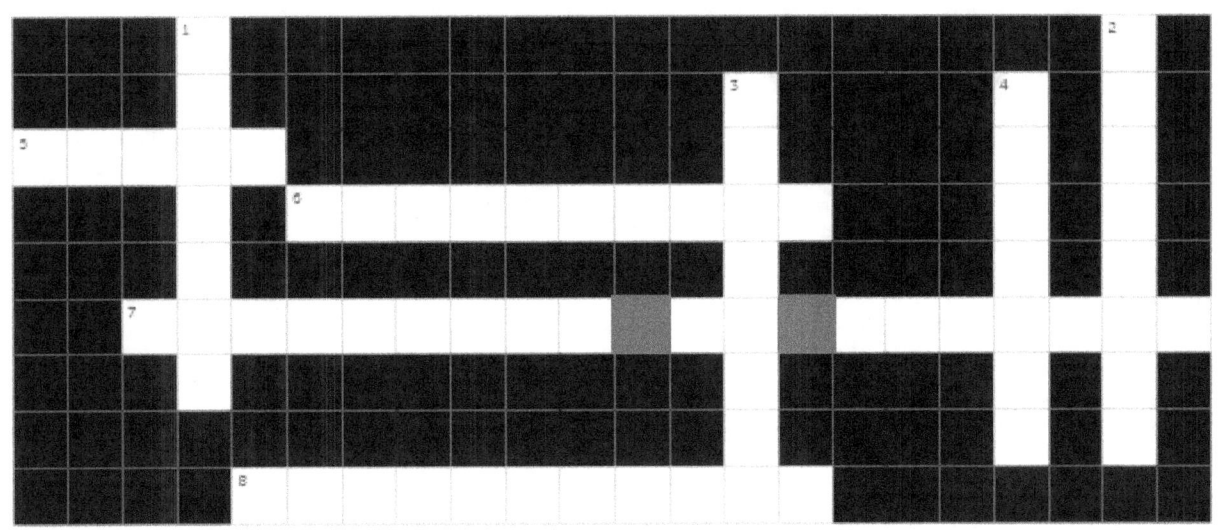

Across

5) Robert and his brave crew were awarded _____ for capturing the Confederate ship.

6) Robert won his election as a _____ to the South Carolina Legislature and the United States House of Representatives during the Reconstruction era.

7) Robert was appointed U.S. _____ in Beaufort, South Carolina

8) Robert replaced the _____ flag with a white flag as the ship came upon the Union Navy.

Down

1) When Robert got his _____ ,he went back to Beaufort and bought the home of his former slave master.

2) Robert worked as a _____ on the confederate ships when he was a slave.

3) Robert was born in _____, South Carolina

4) Robert escaped to the North on the CSS _____.

What are the different branches of the military?

What would motivated you to join the military?

What branch of the military would you join?

Directions: Unscramble the words below about Robert. See if you can get the bonus word.

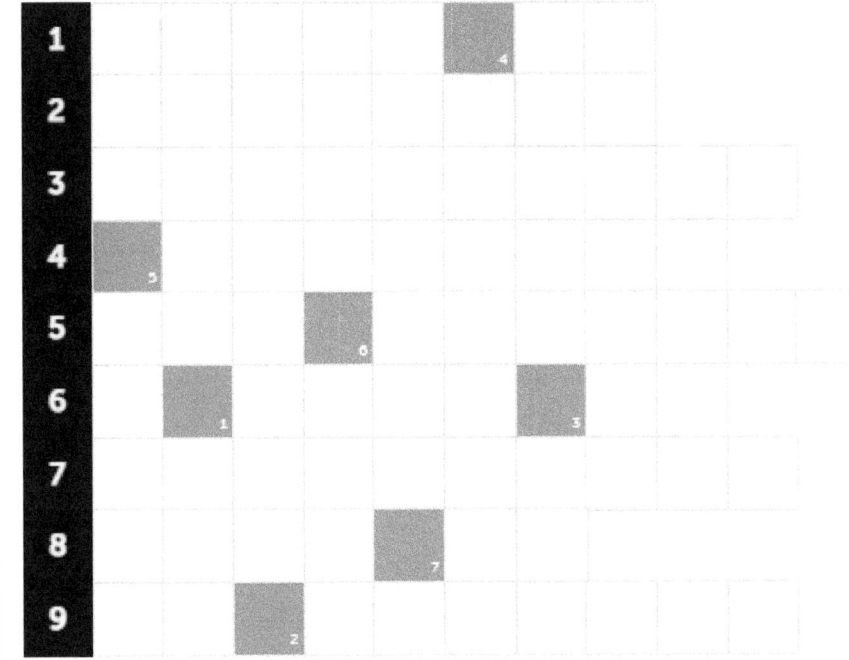

BONUS WORD

1	2	3	4	5	6	7

Unscramble Words

1) toefaBur   **2)** aricilvw   **3)** cariubnpel

4) aunorinmy   **5)** tpeircnelndsniol   **6)** iherupbsl

7) optlniiiac   **8)** selyrva   **9)** talnpsercs

Directions: This is the WGLT Challenge. Solve the cryptogram. As the puzzle solver, you need to find which number belongs to which character. And this can be pretty challenging! You will need to match the number with the letter. There are some letters given to you below. This will help you solve the other words and unlock more characters. **Good Luck.**

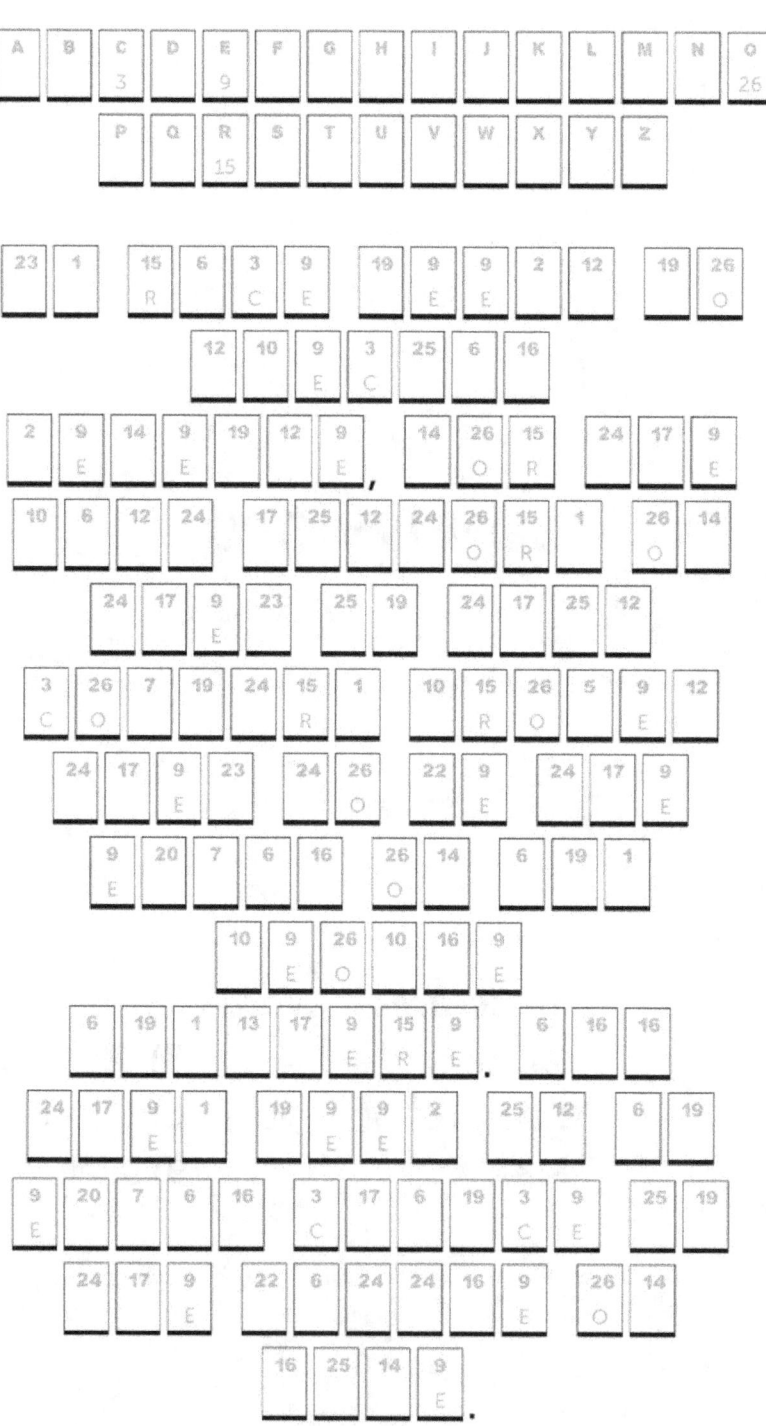

Susie King Taylor

Susie King Taylor

August 6, 1848 – October 6, 1912
NURSE

11

LEFT BLANK ON PURPOSE

Susie King Taylor

Susie King Taylor

Susie King Taylor

Susie King Taylor

Susie King Taylor

Susie King Taylor

Directions: read the bio below and answer the following questions.

Hi, my name is Susie King Taylor. I was born on August 6, 1848, in Liberty County, GA. I was born into slavery and at a young age, I was educated through the "underground education" system. Under Georgia law, it was illegal for enslaved people to be educated. I was educated up until the Civil War started. I fled to St. Catherine's Island to find protection from the Union fleet. I ended up on St. Simon's Island, where Commodore Goldsborough found out that I could read and write. He asked me to create a school for children on the island. I was 13 when I founded the first free African American school for children. I also became the first African American woman to teach a free school in Georgia. While serving with the regiment, I also helped the wounded and tried to alleviate any pain they may have had. I also helped treat smallpox with the use of sassafras tea, which, if drank consistently, would help ward off the terrible disease. I was the first Black nurse to serve in the American Civil War.

1. I founded the first free African-American school for?
   A. Everybody
   B. Children
   C. Adults
2. I help in the recovery of _____ as a nurse in the Civil War?
   A. Smallpox
   B. Chickenpox
   C. Polio
3. I was the first African-American woman to do what?
   A. Teach a free nursing school in Georgia
   B. Teach a free school in Georgia
   C. Teach a free school in Alabama

Directions: Find the words associated with Susie's life and career.

R	C	A	P	T	A	I	N	W	H	I	T	M	O	R	E	I	C
C	E	J	M	E	M	O	I	R	S	W	C	T	J	G	D	Z	I
N	O	C	E	W	C	G	Y	A	T	V	I	Z	H	Z	D	E	V
M	V	L	O	U	B	D	T	X	E	M	D	P	H	Z	S	O	I
V	R	B	O	N	B	Z	V	B	A	L	P	Z	I	R	D	U	L
N	S	P	L	R	S	K	C	Z	C	F	U	E	U	R	Z	G	W
T	I	U	O	P	E	T	V	R	H	W	V	N	X	G	Y	U	A
U	A	M	R	X	L	D	R	V	E	N	I	D	K	A	O	L	R
F	H	N	W	Z	B	D	T	U	R	W	L	H	N	Z	E	L	Q
S	U	D	X	O	Z	C	Y	R	C	T	C	H	I	E	B	A	B
A	R	Z	A	I	K	H	I	M	O	T	R	X	P	Z	F	H	G
V	I	H	B	H	K	A	E	V	R	O	I	M	L	P	E	W	P
A	A	W	M	A	N	B	Q	Y	O	A	P	O	D	Y	D	M	C
N	U	Q	Y	C	X	V	C	I	Y	T	N	S	N	P	C	K	G
N	L	A	Y	J	E	T	U	O	L	V	I	O	Q	E	Q	G	I
A	L	V	B	V	S	X	O	H	S	U	X	X	I	W	R	C	U
H	V	Z	N	D	F	J	P	H	P	Z	I	R	B	N	L	A	X
K	S	M	F	S	O	V	F	Z	G	H	C	Z	V	Q	U	D	G

Find These Words

NURSE   CIVILWAR   GULLAH

TEACHER   MEMOIRS   SAVANNAH

UNIONARMY   CAPTAINWHITMORE   COLOREDTROOPS

RECONSTRUCTIONERA

Would you rather be an officer or enlisted member of the military?

What are some of the key skills and qualities needed for military service?

In what ways does the military help shape your sense of discipline and responsibility?

Directions: Read and answer the questions below. There are clues in the puzzle to help you. Try and solve the cryptic message.

Clue for cryptic message: Susie helped during this time.

Questions

1) The Union Army decided to classify escaped slaves as "_____ of war." They supported the Union Army mainly by working as laborers.

2) Susie was born into slavery on August 6, 1848, at the Great _____.

3) Susie was about ____ when she was encouraged to learn to read and write by her grandmother.

4) Georgia had severe ____ on education for freed and enslaved African Americans back in mid-1800s.

5) Susie surpassed the level of _____ of her first teachers in Georgia by the time Civil War started.

6) Susie taught reading and ____ to upwards of 40 children and even more adults who came to her schoolhouse at night.

7) Susie traveled to Boston as a domestic ____ of a wealthy white family in the 1870s.

8) Susie returned to Savannah and established a school for the _____ children in 1866.

Directions: This is the WGLT Challenge. Solve the cryptogram. As the puzzle solver, you need to find which number belongs to which character. And this can be pretty challenging! You will need to match the number with the letter. There are some letters given to you below. This will help you solve the other words and unlock more characters. **Good Luck.**

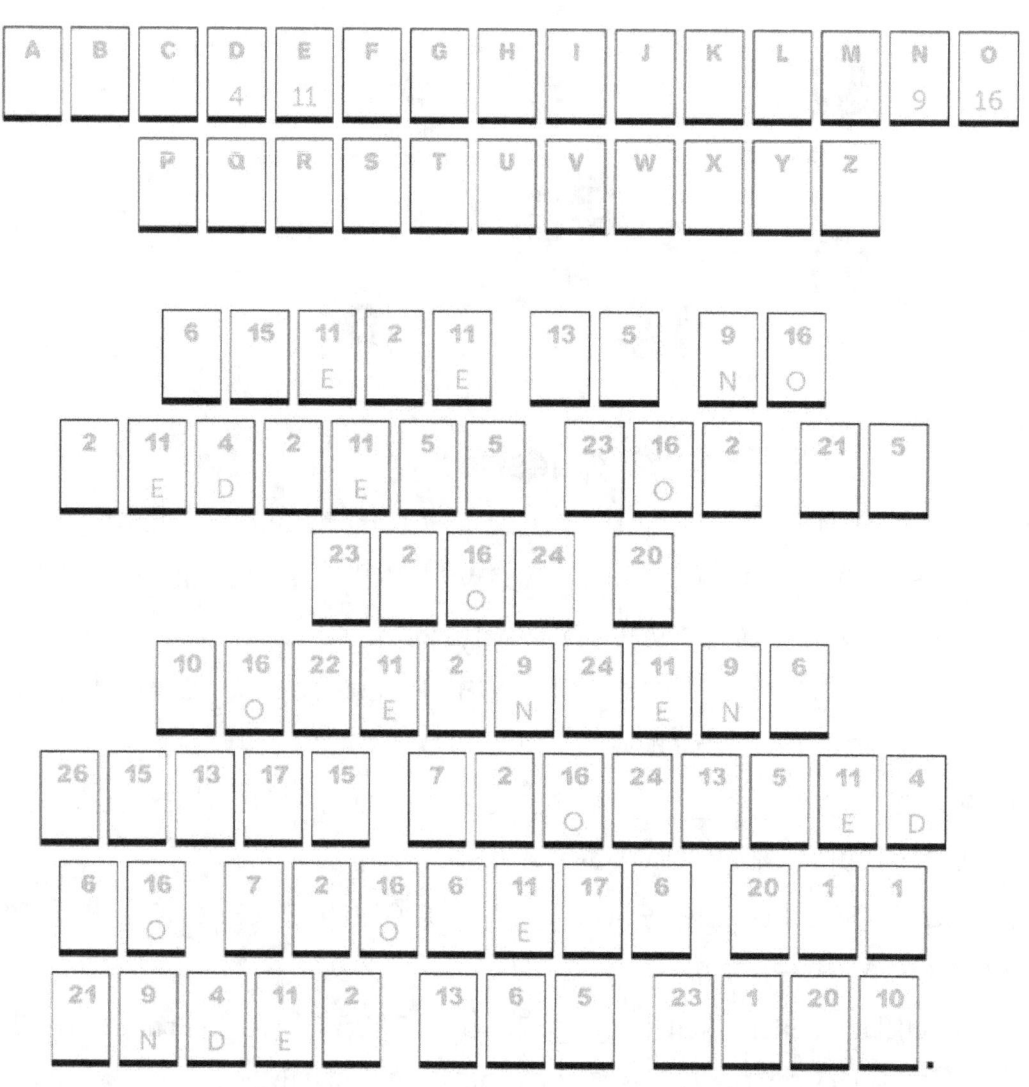

Charles McGee

Charles McGee

December 7, 1919 – January 16, 2022
FIGHTER PILOT

19

LEFT BLANK ON PURPOSE

Charles McGee

Charles McGee

Charles McGee

Charles McGee

Charles McGee

Charles McGee

Hi, my name is Charles McGee. I was born on December 7, 1919, in Cleveland, OH. In 1942, I was attending the University of Illinois to study engineering when World War II broke out. I also became a member of the Alpha Phi Alpha fraternity at that time. I enlisted in the United States Army in 1942 and after that, I earned my pilot's wings and graduated in 1943. I became a part of the Tuskegee Airmen. In 1944, I was stationed in Italy with the 332nd Fighter Group. The aircraft that I flew were the Bell P-39Q Airacobra, the Republic P-47D Thunderbolt and the North American P-51 Mustang fighter aircraft. By the end of 1944, I had flown a total of 137 combat missions and returned to the United States to become an instructor for the North American B-25 Mitchell bombers that were flown by the 477th Bomb Group, which was another unit of the Tuskegee Airmen. The Tuskegee Airmen's success during the war made it possible for President Harry Truman to sign Executive Order 9981 in 1948, which ended racial segregation in the United States Armed Forces.

1. What branch of the military did I join?
   A. United States Navy
   B. United States Army
   C. United States Air Force
2. Which aircraft didn't I pilot?
   A. Bell P-39Q Airacobra
   B. Republic P-47D Thunderbolt
   C. Boeing B-17 Flying Fortress
3. What fraternity did I belong to?
   A. Alpha Phi Alpha
   B. Omega Psi Phi
   C. Phi Beta Sigma

Directions: Answer the questions, to solve the crossword puzzle. You can use the internet if you get stuck on any question.

Across

6) Charles was one of the first pilots to graduate from the Army's experimental program at _____ in June 1943.

7) Charles first began his career in World War II flying with the _____.

8) Charles retired from the U.S. Air Force at the rank of _____.

Down

1) Charles flew P-51 _____ during the Korean War while in the 67th Fighter Bomber Squadron, completing 100 missions.

2) Charles flew more _____ missions in World War II, Korea and Vietnam than any other Air Force pilot.

3) Charles was inducted into the National _____ Hall of Fame.

4) President Trump honored Charles with promotion to the rank of _____ general.

5) Charles served as the _____ of the Kansas City airport.

How do you think the military contributes to national security and defense?

How does the military fostered a sense of camaraderie and teamwork among its members?

Do you know anyone who has served in the military? If so, which branch?

Directions: Unscramble the words below about Charles. See if you can get the bonus word.

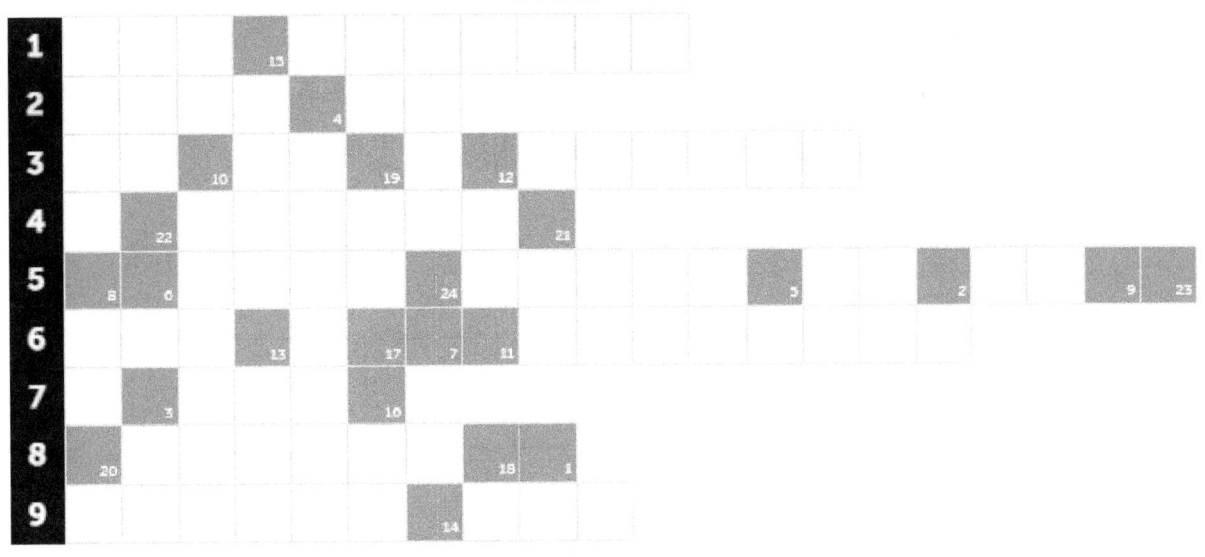

BONUS WORD

Unscramble Words

1) wwrtoorwald **2)** votaria **3)** seeeuitkemarng

4) krrwaaone **5)** ileunisniiyitosorflv **6)** reg3go2trhfpdu3i

7) raymus **8)** nvaellecd **9)** ftlafuwfef

Directions: This is the WGLT Challenge. Solve the cryptogram. As the puzzle solver, you need to find which number belongs to which character. And this can be pretty challenging! You will need to match the number with the letter. There are some letters given to you below. This will help you solve the other words and unlock more characters. **Good Luck.**

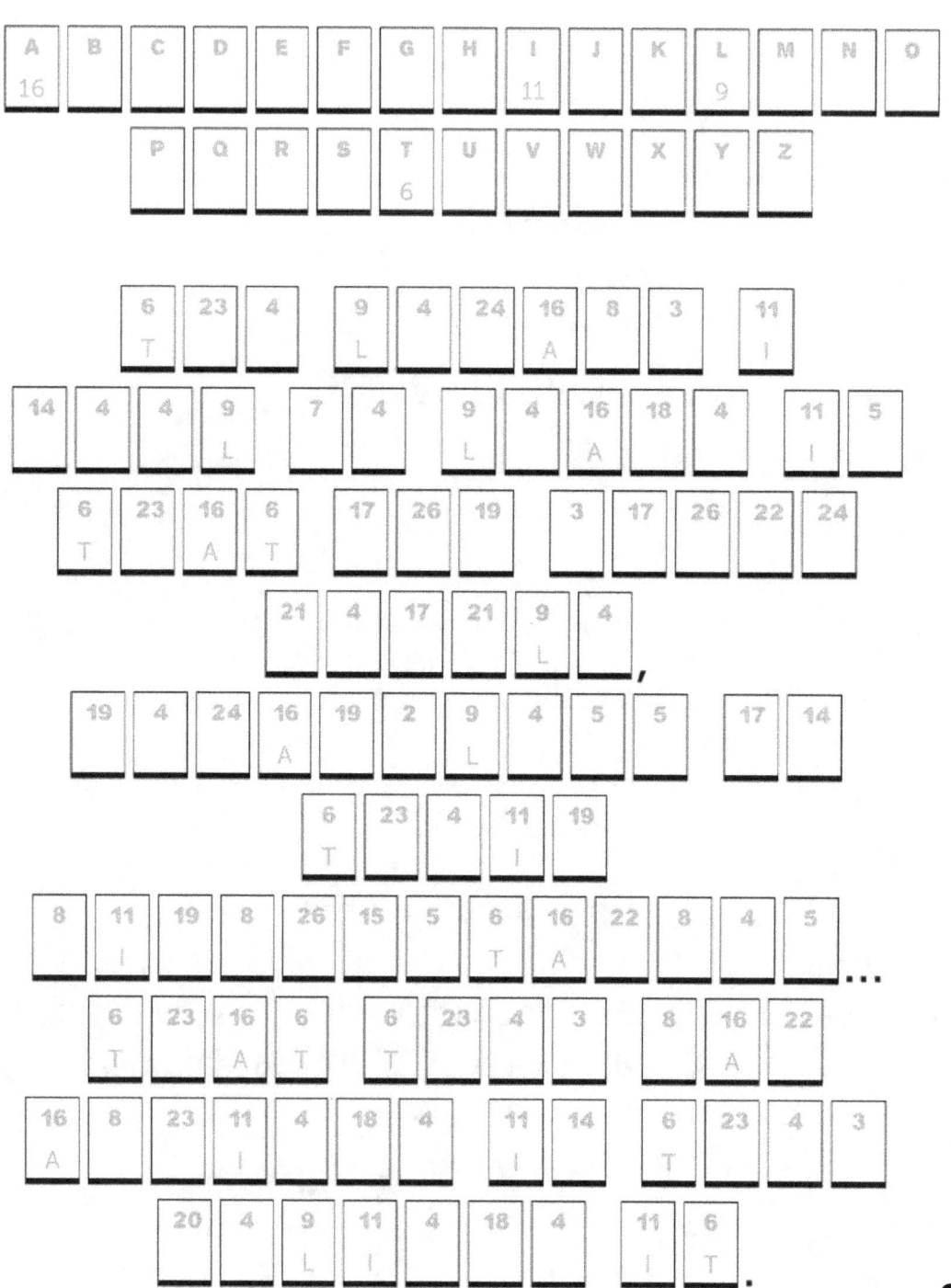

A	B	C	D	E	F	G	H	I	J	K	L	M	N	O
16								11			9			

P	Q	R	S	T	U	V	W	X	Y	Z
				6						

6 23 4 | 9 4 24 16 8 3 | 11
T ... L ... A I

14 4 4 9 | 7 4 | 9 4 16 18 4 | 11 5
... ... L ... ... L ... A I

6 23 16 6 | 17 26 19 | 3 17 26 22 24
T ... A T ... ...

21 4 17 21 9 4,
... ... L ...

19 4 24 16 19 2 9 4 5 5 | 17 14
... ... A ... ... L ... ...

6 23 4 11 19
T ... I

8 11 19 8 26 15 5 6 16 22 8 4 5 ...
... I ... ... T A ... ...

6 23 16 6 | 6 23 4 3 | 8 16 22
T A T T ... ... A ...

16 8 23 11 4 18 4 | 11 14 | 6 23 4 3
A ... I ... ... I T ...

20 4 9 11 4 18 4 | 11 6.
... L I ... I T

Josephine Baker

Josephine Baker

June 3, 1906 - April 12 1975
SPY

Josephine Baker

Josephine Baker

Josephine Baker

Josephine Baker

Josephine Baker

Josephine Baker

Hi, my name is Freda Josephine McDonald. I was born on June 3, 1906, in St. Louis, MO. After several auditions, I secured a role in the chorus line of a touring production of the groundbreaking and hugely successful Broadway revue Shuffle Along. I was 13. The show shut down in 1925, so I sailed to Paris. I had a successful tour and I returned to France in 1926 to star in the Folies Bergère. After many years of success in France, World War II broke out and I was recruited by the Deuxième Bureau, which was the French military intelligence agency, as an "honorable correspondent." Essentially, I was a spy for the French. I joined an all-female group in the Free French Forces Air Force with the rank of second lieutenant. I worked with Jacques Abtey, who was the head of French counterintelligence in Paris. After the war, I was awarded the Resistance Medal by the French Committee of National Liberation and the Croix de Guerre by the French military and was named a Chevalier of the Légion d'honneur by General Charles de Gaulle.

1. What musical was I apart of when I was a young teen?
   A. Exposition des Arts Décoratifs
   B. The Chocolate Dandies
   C. Shuffle Along
2. What was my rank in the Free French Forces Air Force?
   A. 2nd Lieutenant
   B. 1st Lieutenant
   C. Major
3. Who was I a spy for?
   A. United States
   B. French
   C. Germany

Directions: Find the words associated with Josephine's life and career.

T	T	Z	E	E	E	H	S	N	U	N	L	F	F	Q	O	I	E
H	A	R	L	E	M	R	E	N	A	I	S	S	A	N	C	E	D
J	N	W	O	S	R	J	L	T	V	I	D	Z	U	X	F	S	B
L	Q	D	H	I	U	E	W	H	F	M	P	G	W	T	C	O	Y
V	H	P	G	R	T	H	C	K	O	Q	O	R	X	K	I	D	O
H	S	Y	F	A	L	D	S	N	K	C	I	R	V	R	V	Y	W
L	F	Y	I	P	S	I	L	X	A	D	S	U	A	R	I	O	T
Y	B	R	Z	L	L	S	X	D	L	D	I	I	I	Z	L	P	R
O	Y	L	C	J	Z	R	K	Y	P	C	N	J	A	U	R	M	A
F	L	C	X	C	A	K	K	J	Y	B	G	K	Y	J	I	L	W
A	J	K	H	Y	A	Z	Z	Y	O	Z	E	J	X	V	G	M	D
D	K	U	N	I	V	X	Z	W	W	D	R	O	R	K	H	N	L
G	A	B	D	I	C	C	T	A	I	A	F	C	F	U	T	Y	R
S	A	I	V	R	D	R	P	S	G	O	V	H	U	W	S	A	O
T	V	K	K	H	I	K	P	R	A	E	S	T	O	X	R	I	W
W	Q	H	A	B	M	Y	M	A	I	G	Z	D	K	H	I	K	I
P	U	G	E	O	K	I	K	J	E	V	K	K	P	T	D	B	K
O	Y	S	E	I	T	N	E	W	T	G	N	I	R	A	O	R	Q

Find These Words

JAZZAGE	SINGER	HARLEMRENAISSANCE
DANCER	SPY	WORLDWARTWO
PARIS	CIVILRIGHTS	RAINBOWTRIBE
ROARINGTWENTIES		

Which military branch is considered to be the best? Why do you fell that way?

What values and principles does the military branch prioritize?

Can you describe a time when you witnessed the impact of a military's work on local communities

Directions: Read and answer the questions below. There are clues in the puzzle to help you. Try and solve the cryptic message.

Clue for cryptic message: Josephine liked doing this.

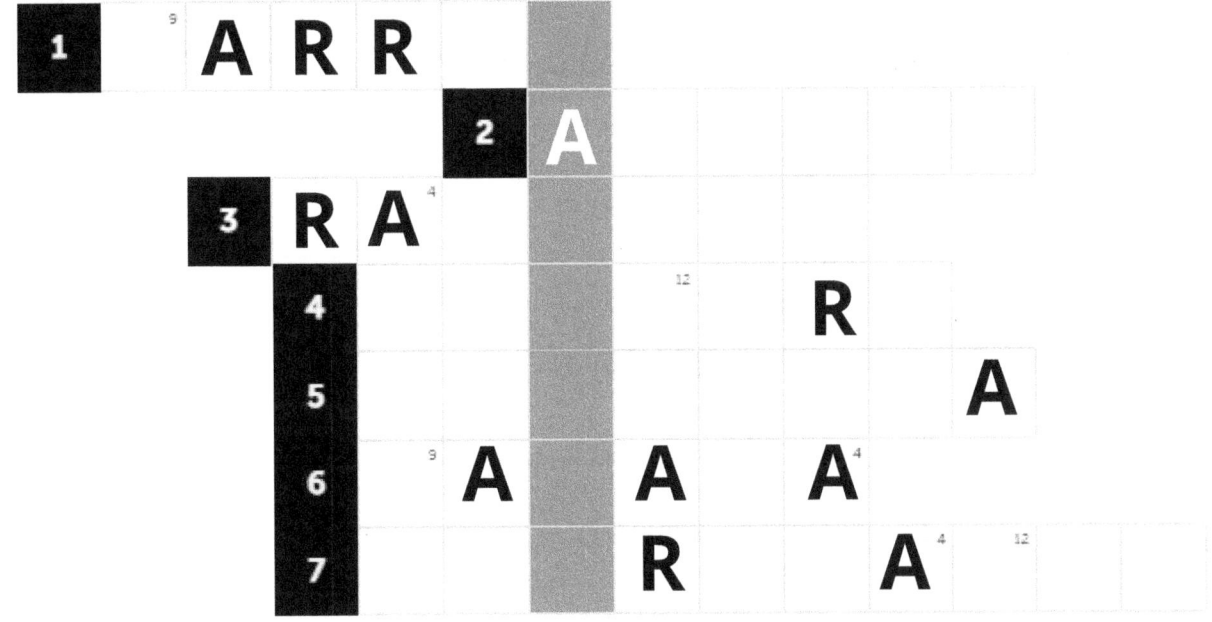

Questions

1) Josephine was _____ entry to the United States for ten years.

2) Josephine was a spy for the _____ forces during World War II.

3) Josephine adopted twelve children of different races and dubbed them "The ____ Tribe."

4) Josephine was the first black woman to star in a major motion _____.

5) Josephine had a cheetah named _____ that was originally part of her dance performance.

6) Josephine signature dance was dubbed the "_____ dance" partly for the risky outfit she wore when dancing.

7) Josephine refused to perform in front of _____ audiences and gave speeches on the problem of racism.

Directions: This is the WGLT Challenge. Solve the cryptogram. As the puzzle solver, you need to find which number belongs to which character. And this can be pretty challenging! You will need to match the number with the letter. There are some letters given to you below. This will help you solve the other words and unlock more characters. **Good Luck.**

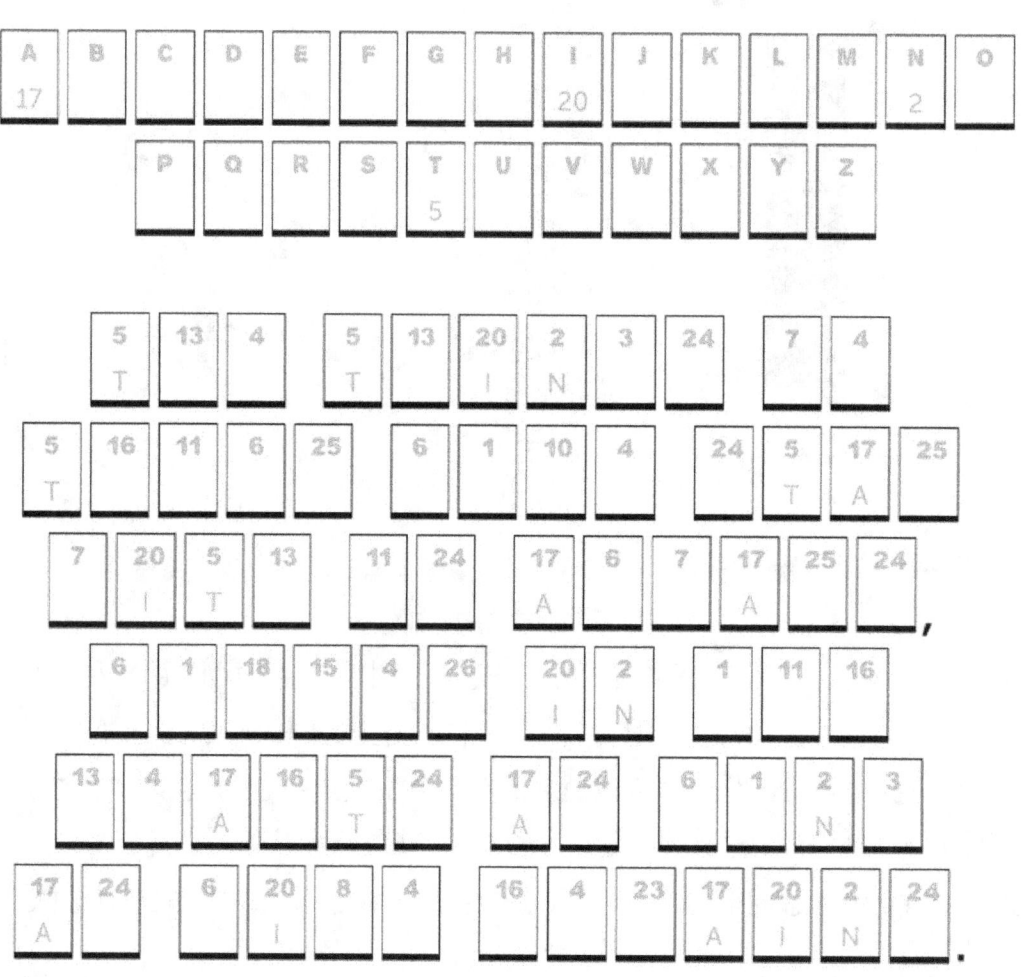

William Johnson

William Johnson

July 15, 1892 – July 1, 1929
SOLDIER

35

LEFT BLANK ON PURPOSE

William Johnson

William Johnson

William Johnson

William Johnson

William Johnson

William Johnson

Hi, my name is William Henry Johnson. I was born on July 15, 1892, in Winston-Salem, NC. In 1917, I enlisted in the United States Military by joining the all-Black New York National Guard 15th Infantry Regiment, which was redesignated as the 369th Infantry Regiment. My regiment was also known as the "Harlem Hellfighters." We joined the 185th Infantry Brigade upon arrival in France. We were then loaned to the 161st Division of the French Army. Our regiment was assigned to Outpost 20 in the Champagne region of France. We were equipped with French rifles and helmets. In 1918, while on observation post duty, I came under attack by a German raiding party of around 36 soldiers. Using grenades, the butt of my rifle, a bolo knife and my bare fists, I repelled the Germans, killing four and wounding others. I rescued a soldier from capture and saved some of my fellow soldiers. I earned the nickname "Black Death." In 1918, the French awarded me with a Croix de Guerre and a star and bronze palm. I was the first U.S. soldier in World War I to receive that honor.

1. What is the nickname of the 369th Infantry Regiment?
   A. Black Death
   B. Harlem Hellfighters
   C. NY Killers
2. What year did I fight off the Germans?
   A. 1918
   B. 1917
   C. 1920
3. I was the first U.S. soldier in World War I to receive?
   A. Purple Heart
   B. Medal of Honor
   C. Croix de guerre

Across

3) Henry was the first American of any race to receive the French _____ with Palme, France's highest award for valor.

5) Henry was a part of the _____ during World War I.

7) Henry was awarded the _____ posthumously by President Obama.

8) Henry fought off a _____ raid in hand-to-hand combat, experiencing 21 wounds.

Down

1) Henry did a tour of speeches around the United States, until black vs white issues on the _____ came up in one of the speeches.

2) Henry was posthumously presented with the _____ by President Clinton.

4) President Roosevelt who eventually called Henry one of the "five ____ Americans" to serve in World War I.

6) Henry has a street named for him in ____, NY, with a monument.

Would you rather be active duty or an reservist in the military?

What's would you want to be in the military? Why?

Do veterans deserve more respect than non-veterans? Why?

Directions: Unscramble the words below about William. See if you can get the bonus word.

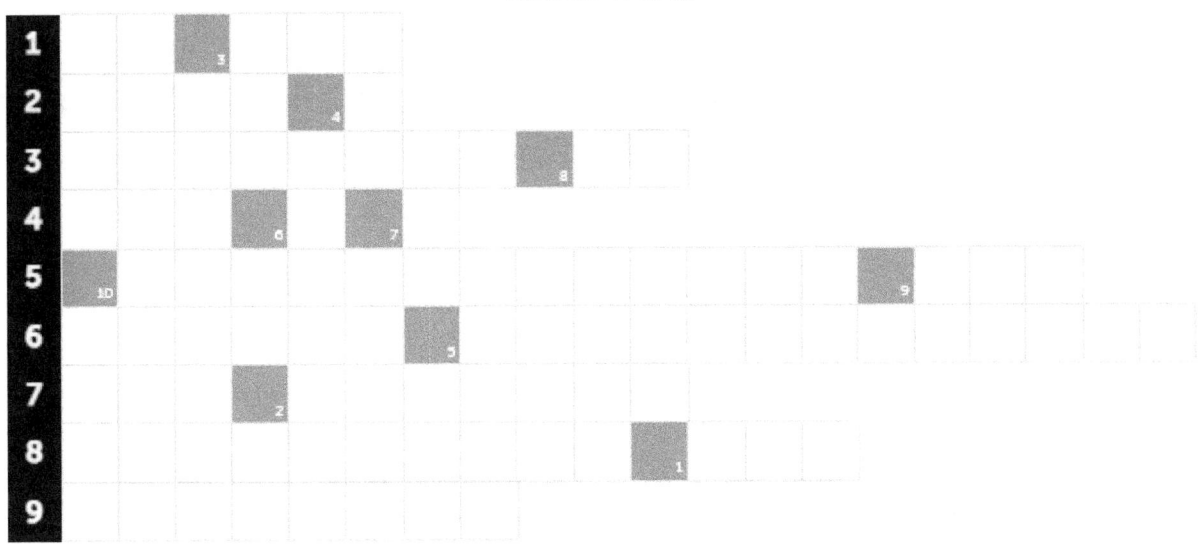

BONUS WORD

1	2	3	4	5	6	7	8	9	10

Unscramble Words

1) ruamsy   **2)** rfcneh   **3)** luephtparre

4) osierdl   **5)** etfherhielaslrlhmg   **6)** kyirwoanuonanealgdtr

7) raelwnoowrd   **8)** eedspnbitaarmo   **9)** tgerenas

Directions: This is the WGLT Challenge. Solve the cryptogram. As the puzzle solver, you need to find which number belongs to which character. And this can be pretty challenging! You will need to match the number with the letter. There are some letters given to you below. This will help you solve the other words and unlock more characters. **Good Luck.**

Harriet West

Harriet West

June 4, 1904 - February 21, 1999
OFFICER 43

Harriet West

Harriet West

Harriet West

Harriet West

Harriet West

Harriet West

Directions: read the bio below and answer the following questions.

Hi, my name is Harriet West. I was born on June 4, 1904, in Jefferson City, MO. I graduated from Kansas State College of Agriculture and Applied Science. In 1942, I entered the military. I started in the Women's Army Corps (WAC). I graduated from The Adjutant General's School of the Army and was put in charge of 50 civilian typists. We notified families of soldiers who were killed, wounded, or missing in action. In 1943, I made a radio broadcast on behalf of the Army, urging Black women to get into uniform. During World War II, the WAC enlisted 6,500 Black women into the service. The military's policy of segregation forced most enlistees into service as uniformed domestic servants. In 1945, I was promoted to the rank of major. I was then able to take an active role in changing the status of "colored" women in the military. I became an advisor to the Army on racial issues and diversity. Due to my earlier experience serving with Director Mary McLeod Bethune of the Bureau of Negro Affairs, I was promoted to the rank of lieutenant colonel in 1948.

1. Which college did I graduate from?
   A. Kansas State College
   B. University of Kansas
   C. Wichita State University
2. What year did I urge black women to get in uniform?
   A. 1945
   B. 1942
   C. 1943
3. What was my highest rank in the WAC?
   A. First Lieutenant
   B. Lieutenant Colonel
   C. Major

Directions: Find the words associated with Harriet's life and career.

U	T	E	G	Q	Q	J	Z	U	A	S	T	G	C	N	S	X	K
B	W	J	P	U	C	J	E	W	M	O	L	X	K	U	C	K	A
K	V	O	D	X	I	U	J	K	Z	L	U	Q	B	S	Z	M	N
T	E	B	M	O	O	X	P	U	Q	D	P	T	Q	E	A	D	S
R	H	C	T	E	I	U	I	U	Z	I	S	Q	Y	C	U	E	A
A	U	O	B	B	N	Z	Z	A	A	E	Z	T	I	N	J	A	S
V	A	R	G	U	W	S	Y	H	N	R	I	R	O	E	Q	G	S
E	R	P	W	R	M	Z	A	U	D	C	Q	W	C	I	P	S	T
L	U	S	A	A	Z	U	C	R	N	P	T	R	C	C	G	L	A
I	B	C	Z	J	G	V	N	O	M	R	O	Z	R	S	Q	Y	T
N	G	E	N	O	K	G	S	P	A	Y	D	V	R	D	C	C	E
G	X	N	P	L	X	R	N	W	M	Q	C	R	M	E	O	M	C
Q	K	T	M	Y	E	I	D	Q	C	U	T	O	V	I	T	A	O
Y	E	E	M	F	K	L	I	Y	Q	F	Z	W	R	L	U	J	L
G	F	R	F	X	R	R	F	Z	Y	A	B	N	W	P	Q	O	L
Z	S	E	F	O	I	Z	V	P	K	Y	P	S	I	P	S	R	E
I	J	T	W	Y	T	I	L	A	U	Q	E	Q	K	A	L	R	G
Y	L	X	W	V	E	T	W	O	J	V	D	W	J	Y	G	D	E

Find These Words

APPLIEDSCIENCES
WORLDWARTWO
EQUALITY
JOBCORPSCENTER

WOMENSARMYCORPS
SOLDIER
JEFFERSONCITY

MAJOR
TRAVELING
KANSASSTATECOLLEGE

Directions: Read and answer the questions. These are your opinions so the answers will vary.

What role does innovation and technological advancements play within the military?

What's your favorite thing about the military?

Which military branch supports the well-being and welfare of its members the best?

Directions: Read and answer the questions below. There are clues in the puzzle to help you. Try and solve the cryptic message.

Clue for cryptic message: Harriet's helped get them in World War II.

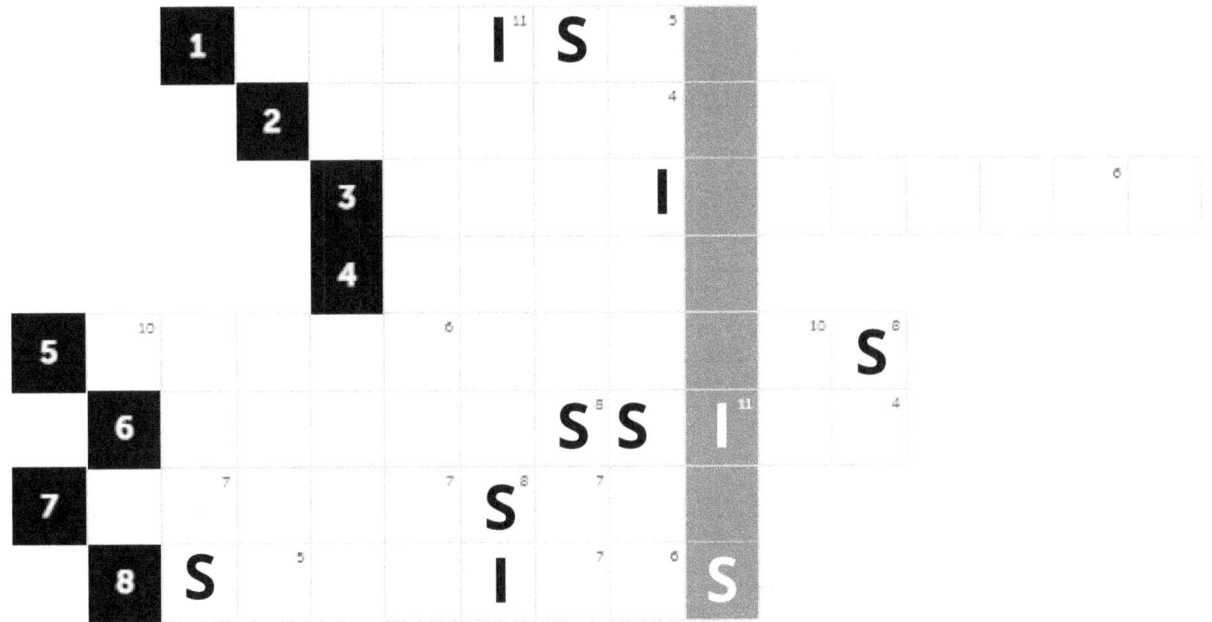

Questions

1) Harriet's goal as an _____ was always to allow her fellow African American women an opportunity to show their abilities.

2) Harriet's title was changed to Lt. _____ once WAC became a part of the Army.

3) Harriet graduated from Kansas State College of _____ and Applied Sciences.

4) Harriet was one of only two African-American women in the WAC to be promoted to the rank of ___.

5) Harriet tried to eliminate references to white and colored from official _____ on information boards.

6) Harriet worked as the aide to Mary McLeod Bethune during the Great _____.

7) Harriet joined the Women's Auxiliary Army Corps to serve her country and _____ her fellow African Americans during World War II.

8) Harriet was in charge of the division that notifies the families of _____ who were killed, wounded, or missing in action.

49

Directions: This is the WGLT Challenge. Solve the cryptogram. As the puzzle solver, you need to find which number belongs to which character. And this can be pretty challenging! You will need to match the number with the letter. There are some letters given to you below. This will help you solve the other words and unlock more characters. **Good Luck.**

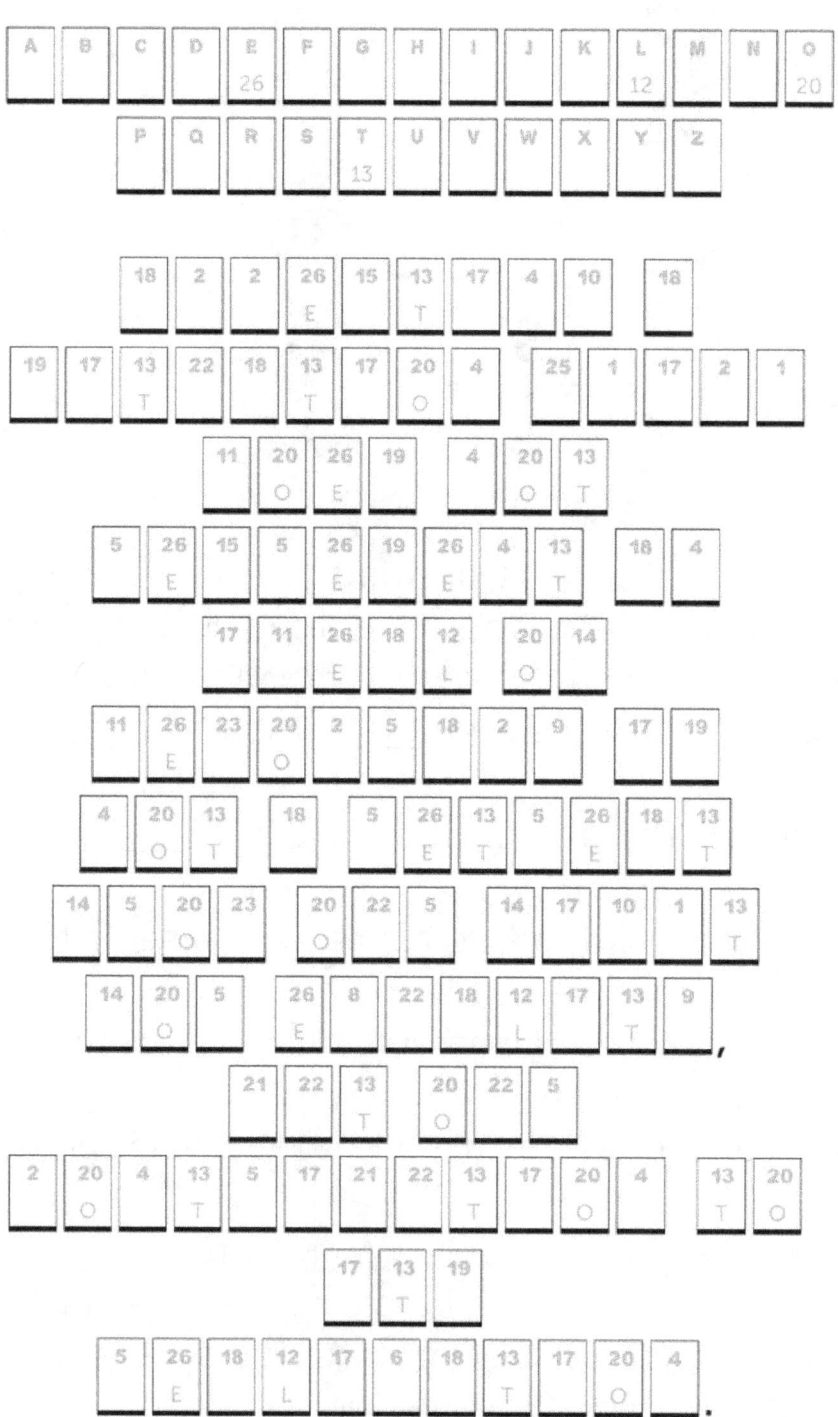

Colin Powell

Colin Powell

April 5, 1937 – October 18, 2021
OFFICER

51

Colin Powell

Colin Powell

Colin Powell

Colin Powell

Colin Powell

Colin Powell

Hi, my name is Colin Powell. I was born on April 5, 1937, in Harlem, NY. I graduated from Morris High School and later graduated from City College of New York (CCNY) with a Bachelor of Science in Geology. I graduated from George Washington University with my Master of Business Administration. I joined the Reserve Officers' Training Corps (ROTC) while I was a student at CCNY. After I graduated, I received a commission as an Army second lieutenant. I served two tours in Vietnam from 1962 to 1963 and 1968. During my first tour, while I was on patrol in an area that was held by the Viet Cong, I was wounded by stepping on a punji stake. I returned as an assistant chief of staff of operations in 1968. I was a professional soldier for 35 years. During this time, I held many command and staff positions and rose to the rank of four-star general. I was a commander of the U.S. Army Forces Command in 1989. In 2001, I became the first African American Secretary of State.

1. Which college did I get my Masters from?
   A. City College of New York
   B. Reserve Officers Training Corps
   C. George Washington University
2. What year did I become Secretary of State?
   A. 2005
   B. 2001
   C. 1989
3. What my highest rank in the military?
   A. Lieutenant General
   B. Brigadier General
   C. General

Directions: Answer the questions, to solve the crossword puzzle. You can use the internet if you get stuck on any question.

Across

3) Colin served as the 12th Chairman of the Joint _____.

5) Colin oversaw U.S. military operations during the _____ Gulf War.

6) Colin joined the Reserve Officers' _____ while attending City College of New York.

7) Colin served as the 65th United States _____.

Down

1) Colin served twice in the _____ War.

2) Colin served as national security advisor under President _____.

4) Colin earned the Soldier's Medal for surviving a _____ crash during the Vietnam War

6) Colin was awarded the Presidential Medal of Freedom _____.

Directions: Read and answer the questions. These are your opinions so the answers will vary.

How does the military promote diversity and inclusion among its ranks?

How has the military influenced your perspective on service to the nation?

What is one aspect of the military you wish more people understood or appreciated?

Directions: Unscramble the words below about Colin. See if you can get the bonus word.

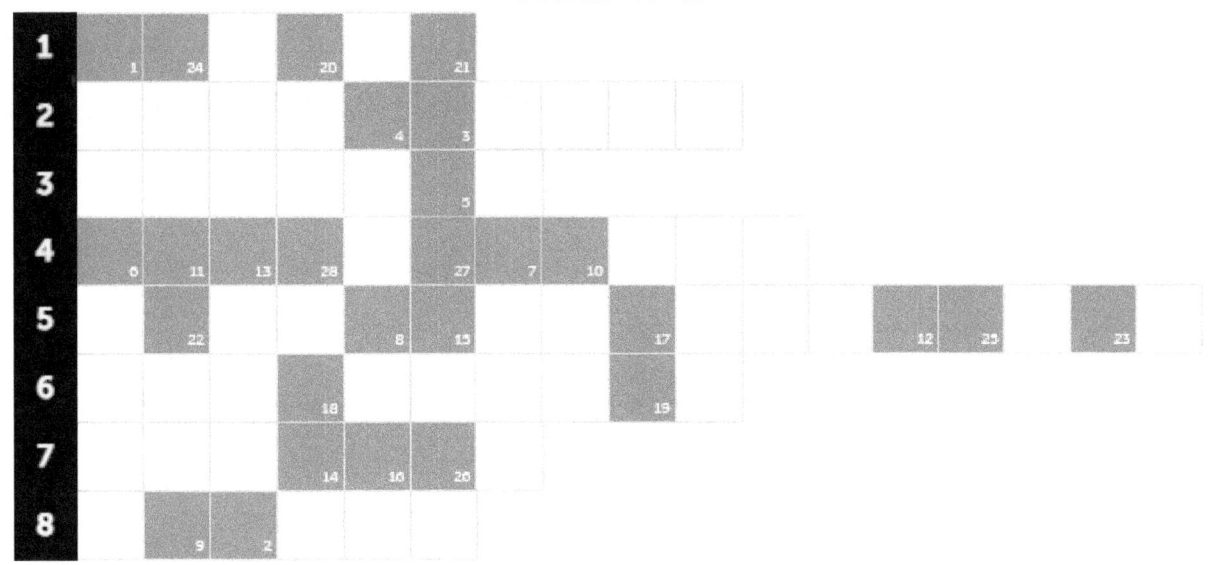

BONUS WORD

Unscramble Words

1) ymruas **2)** itiipancol **3)** feicrof

4) dtsteesrmro **5)** jtheastfnoififofc **6)** nemrvatwia

7) gnreeal **8)** rreang

Directions: This is the WGLT Challenge. Solve the cryptogram. As the puzzle solver, you need to find which number belongs to which character. And this can be pretty challenging! You will need to match the number with the letter. There are some letters given to you below. This will help you solve the other words and unlock more characters. **Good Luck.**

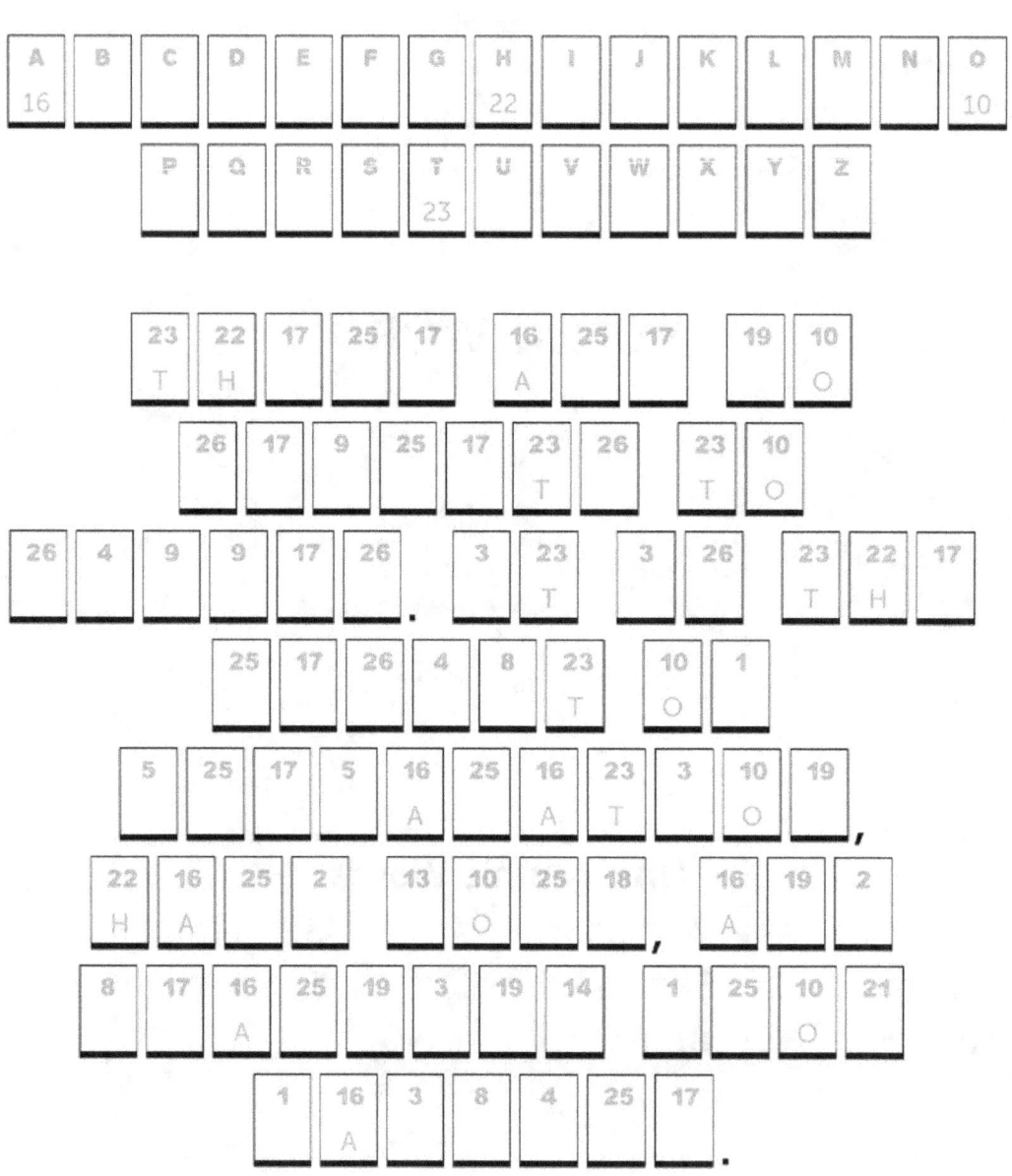

Lorna Mahlock

Lorna Mahlock

1968 – PRESENT
OFFICER

LEFT BLANK ON PURPOSE

Lorna Mahlock

Lorna Mahlock

Lorna Mahlock

Lorna Mahlock

Lorna Mahlock

Lorna Mahlock

Hi, my name is Lorna M. Mahlock. I was born in 1968 in Kingston, Jamaica. I went to an all-girls Catholic school in the Caribbean. I graduated from Marquette University. I enlisted in the United States Marine Corps. I was selected for the Marine Corps Enlisted Commissioning Education Program and I was commissioned in December 1991. I have a master's degree in adult and higher education from the University of Oklahoma at Norman, a master's in national security and strategic studies with distinction from the Naval War College, a master's in strategic studies from the United States Army War College and a master's certificate in information operations from the Naval Postgraduate School. In 2018, I became the first Black woman to be nominated for promotion to brigadier general in the United States Marine Corps (USMC). As a brigadier general, I serve as a deputy commandant for information by leading the Office of the Chief Information Officer for the Marine Corps.

1. What year did I get my commission?
   A. 2018
   B. 1985
   C. 1991
2. Which college didn't I go to?
   A. University of Oklahoma
   B. University of New York
   C. Marquette University
3. I was the first black woman to do what?
   A. Promotion to brigadier general in the USMC
   B. Promotion to brigadier general in the USN
   C. Promotion to brigadier general in the USAF

Directions: Find the words associated with Lorna's life and career.

```
Q T Q V M W P Z V S F Y X W C X J J
N L W C Y G N I W T F A R C R I A T
B R I G A D I E R G E N E R A L U O
O L V T Z P V X S P J N Q A Q G P V
X L Y Y W F V U S J V F H Y N Y L D
W M E T Y C R D K G F O D H V J F H
N M E G E L L O C R A W Y M R A H A
M W S F H O P M D H A U B H N T D W
K R G E M J C V V B Y W Z G A W P P
Q O M T J Z T U S U V N E A U W M A
B G K T S P R O C E N I R A M S H D
O K V E A A T N U Y L G Y I V B Y Z
C M Z U R I F R E P M E S E N W A W
T F E Q L Z N O X X O F F I C E R G
D A F R H C H I E F O F S T A F F K
S L F A A F Q O T S R G W N R N D Z
B T S M X O V Y O X Z P C Z Y Z A C
R L N O I T A I V A D R A W Q A R I
```

Find These Words

OFFICER

SEMPERFI

IRAQWAR

CHIEFOFSTAFF

MARINECORPS

AVIATION

BRIGADIERGENERAL

ARMYWARCOLLEGE

AIRCRAFTWING

MARQUETTE

What advice would you want if you were considering joining the military?

What do you think attracts people to the military?

What specific skills or training can you gained from the military?

Directions: Read and answer the questions below. There are clues in the puzzle to help you. Try and solve the cryptic message.

Clue for cryptic message: Lorna will be this always.

Questions

1) Lorna has a Master's degree in Adult and Higher Education from the University of _____.

2) Lorna was the Air Control Officer G3 Future Operations 1st Marine _____ Wing.

3) Lorna serves as the deputy ___ for combat support of the National Security Agency's Cybersecurity Directorate.

4) Lorna was born in _____, Jamaica.

5) Lorna is a Higher Command and Staff Course graduate of the United _____ Joint Services Command and Staff College.

6) Lorna was the J3 Land Operations Lead and Division _____ Officer, Headquarters European Command.

Directions: This is the WGLT Challenge. Solve the cryptogram. As the puzzle solver, you need to find which number belongs to which character. And this can be pretty challenging! You will need to match the number with the letter. There are some letters given to you below. This will help you solve the other words and unlock more characters. **Good Luck.**

A	B	C	D	E	F	G	H	I	J	K	L	M	N	O
9				4							20			

P	Q	R	S	T	U	V	W	X	Y	Z
				11						

18 22 1 | 15 22 7 | 11(T) 26 4(E) 11(T) | 22 1 11(T)

11(T) 22 | 2 7 26 8 2 10 4(E) | 2 21 .

26 22 6 4(E) 11(T) 17 2 7 24 | 26 6 9(A) 20(L) 20(L)

11(T) 17 9(A) 11(T) 2 | 15 22 17 4(E) 20(L) 8 26

22 10 | 6 9(A) 14 4(E) 26 | 9(A)

15 2 21 21 4(E) 10 4(E) 7 16 4(E) ,

11(T) 4(E) 20(L) 20(L) 6 4(E) | 19 17 9(A) 11(T) 2 11(T)

2 26 | 9(A) 7 15 2 20(L) 20(L) 15 22

6 22 10 4(E) 22 21 2 11(T) .

66

Lucius Theus

Lucius Theus

October 11, 1922 – October 15, 2007
OFFICER

67

LEFT BLANK ON PURPOSE

Lucius Theus

Lucius Theus

Lucius Theus

Lucius Theus

Lucius Theus

Lucius Theus

Directions: read the bio below and answer the following questions.

Hi, my name is Lucius Theus. I was born on October 11, 1922, in Madison County, TN. I graduated from Community High School. I have a Bachelor of Science degree from the University of Maryland and a master's degree in business administration from The George Washington University and I am the first African American graduate of the Harvard Advanced Management Program. I entered the Army Air Corps as a private in December 1942. I stayed enlisted until after World War II. In 1946, I graduated from Officer Candidate School and was commissioned as a second lieutenant. I did a one-year tour of duty as a squadron adjutant at Tuskegee Army Air Field. I fought in the following wars: World War II (1941–1945), the Korean War (1950–1953) and the Vietnam War (1960–1973). I was the first and only mission support officer of the Tuskegee Airmen to be promoted to General and only the third African American in the entire history of the United States Air Force to achieve that rank.

1. What rank did I come in the Air Force as?
   A. 2nd Lieutenant
   B. Private
   C. Private First Class
2. What year did I graduate Officer Candidate School?
   A. 1946
   B. 1942
   C. 1950
3. Which war didn't I fight In?
   A. Korean War
   B. Vietnam War
   C. World War I

Directions: Answer the questions, to solve the crossword puzzle. You can use the internet if you get stuck on any question.

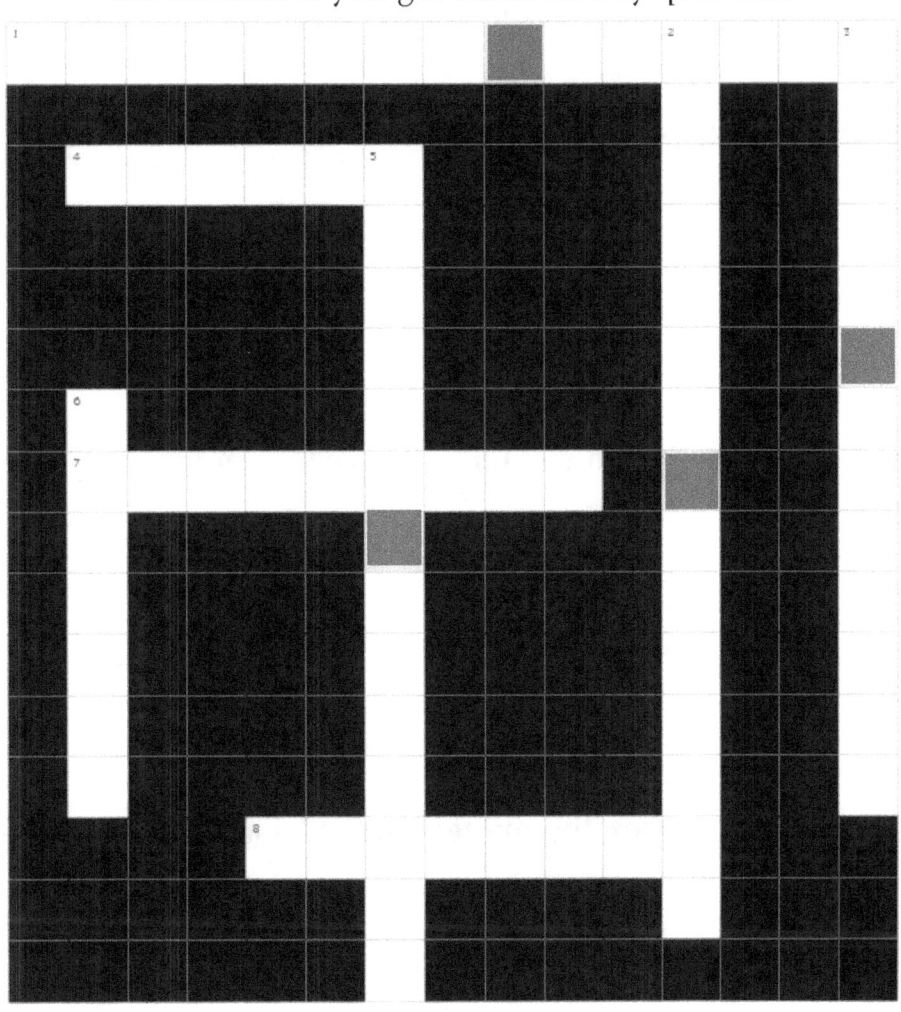

Across

1) Lucius assisted in establishing the _____ of the Tuskegee Airmen in Detroit, MI.

4) Lucius graduated ____ in his class at Officer Candidate School.

7) Lucius led a task force that produced significant DOD race-relations ___ and policies.

8) Lucius was an aviator, who served as a ____ Airman during World War II.

Down

2) Lucius was the first African American _____.

3) Lucius became the third black _____ in the United States Air Force.

5) Lucius developed a ___ system for military payrolls.

6) Lucius was the first African-American combat support officer to be promoted to the rank of ____ officer.

If you could meet a military hero who would it be?

Can you share a moment when you felt a deep sense of pride about a member of the military?

Can you describe a time when the military exceed your own expectations?

Directions: Unscramble the words below about Lucius. See if you can get the bonus word.

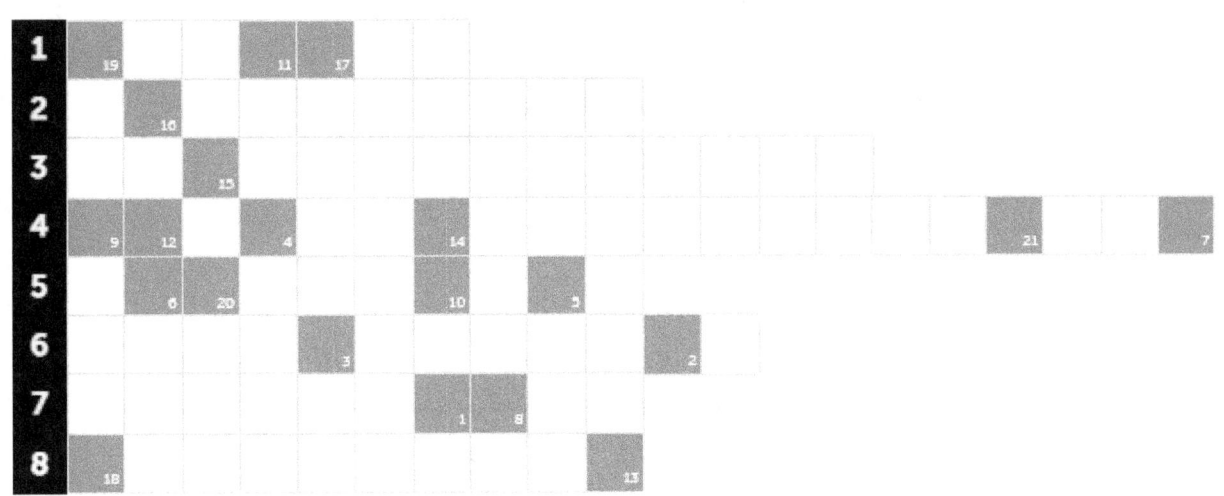

BONUS WORD

Unscramble Words

1) fifcreo

2) ouaeifrrsc

3) miegruentekeas

4) rtleifyrnavsoyuidmna

5) eranbsotrz

6) oaljneregarm

7) myraahacnb

8) emaahfollf

Directions: This is the WGLT Challenge. Solve the cryptogram. As the puzzle solver, you need to find which number belongs to which character. And this can be pretty challenging! You will need to match the number with the letter. There are some letters given to you below. This will help you solve the other words and unlock more characters. **Good Luck.**

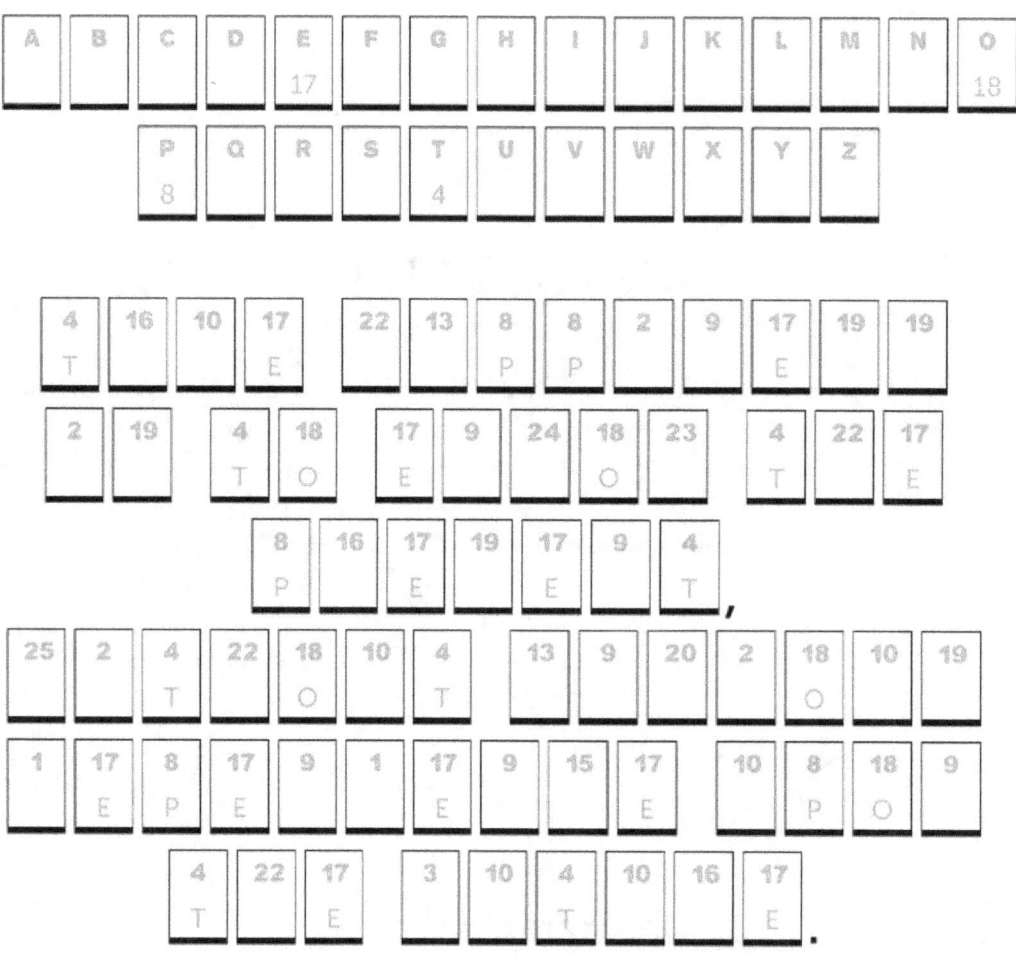

A	B	C	D	E	F	G	H	I	J	K	L	M	N	O
				17										18

P	Q	R	S	T	U	V	W	X	Y	Z
8				4						

Line 1: 4(T) 16 10 17(E) 22 13 8(P) 8(P) 2 9 17(E) 19 19

Line 2: 2 19 4(T) 18(O) 17(E) 9 24 18(O) 23 4(T) 22 17(E)

Line 3: 8(P) 16 17(E) 19 17(E) 9 4(T) ,

Line 4: 25 2 4(T) 22 18(O) 10 4(T) 13 9 20 2 18(O) 10 19

Line 5: 1 17(E) 8(P) 17(E) 9 1 17(E) 9 15 17(E) 10 8(P) 18(O) 9

Line 6: 4(T) 22 17(E) 3 10 4(T) 10 16 17(E) .

Marcelite J. Harris

January 16, 1943 – September 7, 2018
OFFICER

75

LEFT BLANK ON PURPOSE

Marcelite J. Harris

Marcelite J. Harris

Marcelite J. Harris

Marcelite J. Harris

Marcelite J. Harris

Marcelite J. Harris

Directions: read the bio below and answer the following questions.

Hi, my name is Marcelite J. Harris. I was born on January 16, 1943, in Houston, TX. I graduated from Kashmere Gardens High School. I graduated from Spelman College with a bachelor's degree in speech and drama. I completed Officer Training School at Lackland Air Force Base and then joined the Women in the Air Force (WAF) program. I enrolled in the Aircraft Maintenance Officer Course at Chanute Air Force Base in 1970. In 1971, I was named a maintenance supervisor for the 49th Tactical Fighter Squadron at the Korat Royal Thai Air Force Base in Thailand. I was the first female aircraft maintenance officer, one of the first two female air officers to command at the United States Air Force Academy and the Air Force's first female Director of Maintenance. In 1991, I became the first African-American female general officer of the United States Air Force. In 1997, I retired as a major general and as the highest-ranking female officer in the Air Force and the nation's highest-ranking African American woman in the Department of Defense.

1. What college did I get my Bachelors degree from?
   A. Voorhees College
   B. Spelman College
   C. Bennett College
2. What is my highest rank in the Air Force?
   A. Brigadier General
   B. Lieutenant General
   C. Major General
3. I was the first female director of?
   A. Maintenance
   B. Communications
   C. Infantry

Directions: Find the words associated with Marcelite's life and career.

E	L	N	H	G	F	Z	F	R	J	Z	U	V	M	G	F	Q	D
I	D	E	L	T	A	S	I	G	M	A	T	H	E	T	A	K	I
A	C	M	S	P	E	L	M	A	N	C	O	L	L	E	G	E	Y
M	F	A	D	G	Q	R	W	S	M	D	W	W	V	I	R	P	X
A	A	J	Y	W	D	H	E	R	F	P	P	Y	D	G	W	T	B
R	N	O	C	M	Q	W	I	F	C	O	I	D	S	E	M	X	L
D	K	R	B	A	T	W	G	L	N	O	X	B	C	I	X	C	X
D	H	G	I	F	H	O	U	S	T	O	N	N	J	U	C	Y	S
N	G	E	X	U	A	N	Q	F	O	R	A	B	A	H	I	T	S
A	L	N	Z	W	Y	S	A	O	K	N	E	I	R	Q	Q	B	A
H	J	E	V	D	S	F	L	A	E	Y	W	F	N	P	J	Y	S
C	Q	R	R	R	L	C	Z	T	C	Q	Z	U	P	S	Q	K	A
E	Z	A	L	K	F	A	N	W	H	P	F	W	O	K	Y	H	N
E	M	L	X	C	L	I	D	H	J	L	N	I	S	S	M	S	O
P	W	N	Q	Y	A	E	C	R	O	F	R	I	A	S	U	O	S
S	P	I	E	M	K	S	P	T	E	X	R	L	Z	R	R	O	C
S	G	C	L	D	V	Y	A	A	W	W	D	W	P	M	G	K	N
P	F	T	Z	O	B	R	O	N	Z	E	S	T	A	R	J	G	Q

Find These Words

USAIRFORCE   DELTASIGMATHETA   SPELMANCOLLEGE

MAJORGENERAL   NAACP   MAINTENANCE

BRONZESTAR   NASA   HOUSTON

SPEECHANDDRAMA

Directions: Read and answer the questions. These are your opinions so the answers will vary.

What is the motto of your favorite military branch?

What's your favorite thing about the Air Force?

How has the military instilled a sense of duty and loyalty within our country?

Directions: Read and answer the questions below. There are clues in the puzzle to help you. Try and solve the cryptic message.

Clue for cryptic message: Marcelite went here at one point.

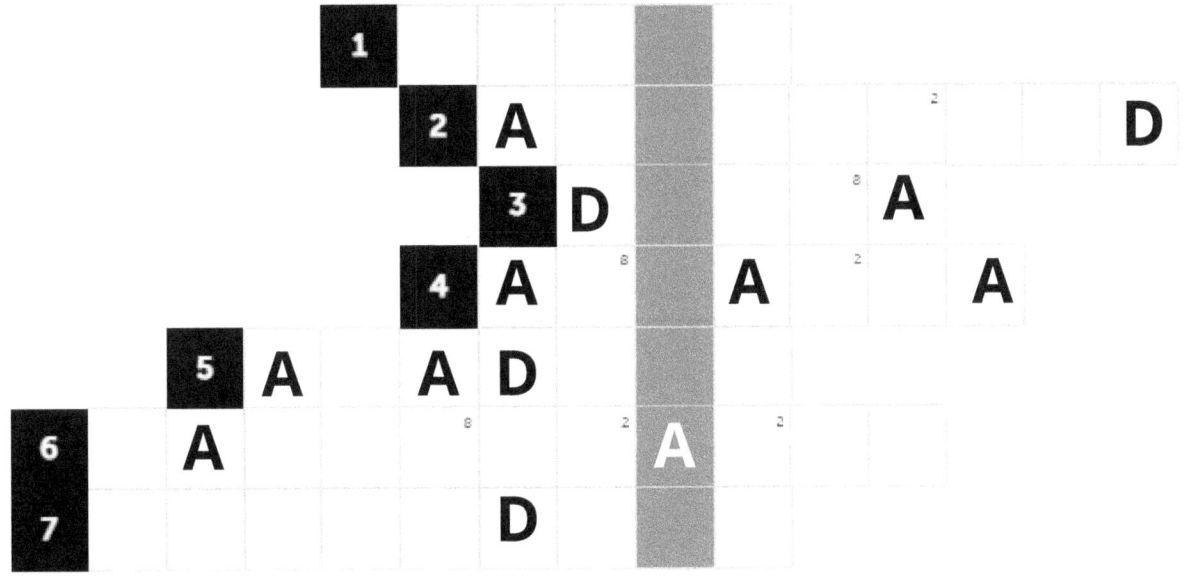

Questions

1) Marcelite was the ___ woman deputy commander for maintenance.

2) Marcelite was ___ by President Obama to serve as a member of the Board of Visitors for the United States Air Force Academy.

3) Marcelite was a member of ___ Sigma Theta sorority.

4) Marcelite was a Treasurer of the ___ Branch of the National Association for the Advancement of Colored People (NAACP).

5) Marcelite one of the first two women air officers commanding at the U.S. Air Force ___.

6) Marcelite was the first woman aircraft _____ officer.

7) Marcelite served as a White House social aide during ____ Carter administration.

Directions: This is the WGLT Challenge. Solve the cryptogram. As the puzzle solver, you need to find which number belongs to which character. And this can be pretty challenging! You will need to match the number with the letter. There are some letters given to you below. This will help you solve the other words and unlock more characters. **Good Luck.**

Benjamin Davis Jr.

Benjamin Davis Jr.

December 18, 1912 – July 4, 2002

OFFICER

LEFT BLANK ON PURPOSE

Benjamin Davis Jr.

Benjamin Davis Jr.

Benjamin Davis Jr.

Benjamin Davis Jr.

Benjamin Davis Jr.

Benjamin Davis Jr.

Hi, my name is Benjamin Oliver Davis Jr. I was born on December 18, 1912, in Washington, D.C. I graduated from Central High School. In 1936, I graduated from the United States Military Academy with a commission as a second lieutenant of infantry. At this time, the Army only had two Black officers who weren't chaplains: Benjamin O. Davis, Sr. (my dad) and me. In May 1941, I entered the Advanced Flying School at the nearby Tuskegee Army Air Base and received my pilot's wings in 1942. My four classmates and I became the first African American combat fighter pilots in the U.S. military. I was the first African American officer to solo an Army Air Corps aircraft. I flew 60 missions in a P-39, Curtiss P-40 and P-47 and P-51 Mustang fighters. Later that year, I was promoted to lieutenant colonel and was named the commander of the first all-Black air unit, the 99th Pursuit Squadron. In 1954, I became the first African American brigadier general in the United States Air Force (USAF).

1. What year did I become a second lieutenant?
   A. 1936
   B. 1942
   C. 1954
2. What aircraft didn't I fly?
   A. P-39
   B. Curtiss P-40
   C. Curtiss P-36 Hawk
3. I was the first African American to do what in the USAF?
   A. Become an Officer
   B. Become a Brigadier General
   C. Become a four start General

Across

1) Benjamin was ___ of the 99th Fighter Squadron and the 332nd Fighter Group during World War II.

4) Benjamin and the 332nd Squadron were Nicknamed the "___" because of the distinctive red paint on their planes.

5) Benjamin's father was the first African American to become a ___ in any branch of the U.S. military.

6) Benjamin was one of the first African-American ___ to see combat.

7) Benjamin led combats in Tunisia in North Africa and ___ missions as a part of Operation Corkscrew in Germany.

8) Benjamin was awarded the Air Force ___ Service Medal.

Down

2) Benjamin escorted bombers on ___ missions over Europe.

3) Benjamin flew sixty missions in P-39, Curtiss P-40, P-47 and P-51 ___ fighters.

If you could go back to any period in time, which would you choose?

What's your favorite thing about the Marine Corps?

What is a unique talent you can get from the military?

Directions: Unscramble the words below about Benjamin. See if you can get the bonus word.

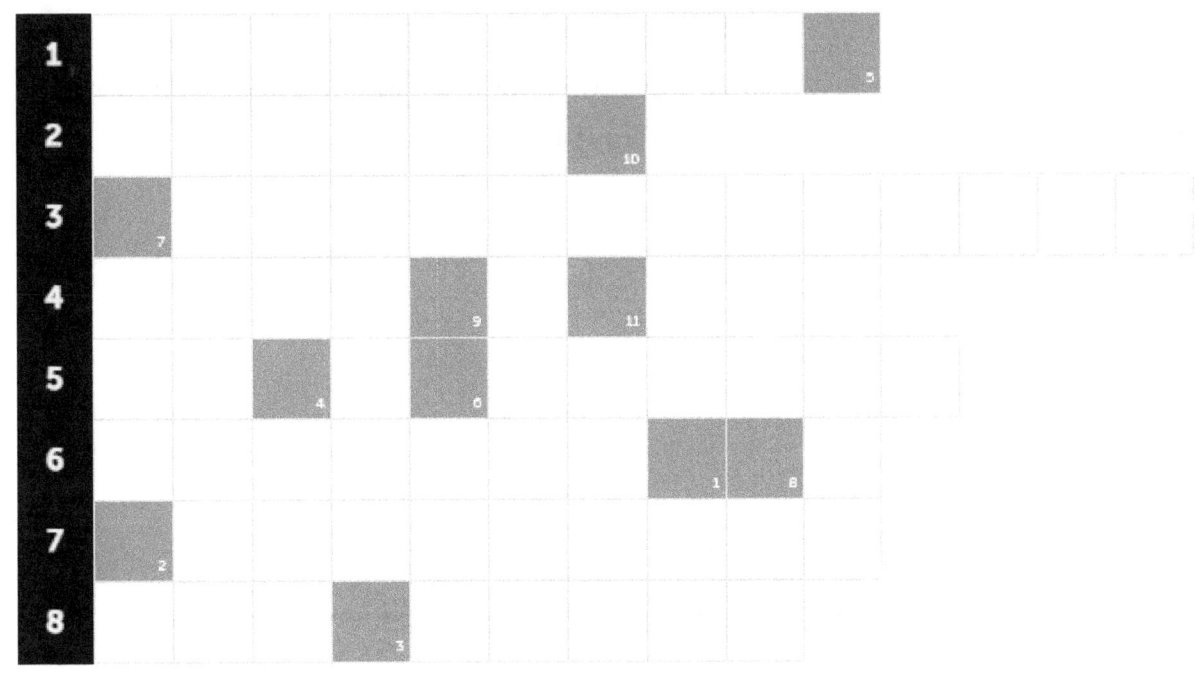

BONUS WORD

1	2	3	4	5	6	7	8	9	10	11

Unscramble Words

1) fsriaoecur

2) nrlgaee

3) ksemgetruieane

4) 4trcsiup0s

5) olrwwrotdaw

6) stesrlivar

7) mllaffaheo

8) waaknreor

Directions: This is the WGLT Challenge. Solve the cryptogram. As the puzzle solver, you need to find which number belongs to which character. And this can be pretty challenging! You will need to match the number with the letter. There are some letters given to you below. This will help you solve the other words and unlock more characters. **Good Luck.**

Cathay Williams

Cathay Williams

September 1844 – 1893
BUFFALO SOLDIER

LEFT BLANK ON PURPOSE

Cathay Williams

Cathay Williams

Cathay Williams

Cathay Williams

Cathay Williams

Cathay Williams

Hi, my name is Cathay Williams. I was born in September 1844 in Independence, MO. In 1861, I was 17 when Union forces occupied Jefferson City during the early stages of the Civil War. After being captured and designated by the Union as "contraband," I was forced to serve in the Union Army as a cook and a washerwoman before I voluntarily enlisted. I wanted to make my own living and not be dependent on relatives or friends. Only my cousin and a friend knew what I was about to do. There was a prohibition against women serving in the military, so in 1866, I enlisted as William Cathay and pawned myself off as a man. I passed a cursory examination because the Army didn't require full medical exams at the time. I was assigned to the 38th U.S. Infantry Regiment. I got small pox and beat it, but afterward, I was frequently hospitalized. The post surgeon finally discovered I was a woman and I was honorably discharged. I was the first Black woman to enlist and the only documented woman to serve in the United States Army during the American Indian Wars.

1. What did I do in the Army before I enlisted?
   A. Cook
   B. Nurse.
   C. Gunner
2. What year did I enlist in the Army?
   A. 1868
   B. 1865
   C. 1866
3. I was the first black woman to do what?
   A. Enlist in the US Navy
   B. Enlist in the US Army
   C. Enlist in the US Air Force

Directions: Find the words associated with Cathay's life and career.

C	N	T	N	E	M	I	G	E	R	Y	R	T	N	A	F	N	I
V	N	N	K	G	I	O	M	U	U	O	M	D	Z	W	Z	C	U
K	G	V	R	E	C	B	N	W	F	H	S	A	R	Q	Y	G	N
K	O	H	S	R	O	W	N	A	F	S	J	O	J	O	O	K	H
Y	R	F	S	E	N	I	Y	L	V	Q	J	D	E	Y	B	L	R
A	Y	I	E	I	T	Z	U	K	Z	N	C	K	W	N	G	W	K
H	B	Q	R	D	R	A	K	O	R	H	D	N	G	P	X	K	P
T	A	X	T	L	A	B	X	F	H	E	C	V	E	N	W	V	K
A	S	W	O	B	L	C	H	H	G	I	V	K	L	I	E	I
C	W	E	M	S	A	S	S	O	P	X	X	D	N	U	O	P	Q
M	U	M	A	O	N	P	D	N	Q	M	U	Y	L	L	E	D	D
A	Z	J	E	L	D	C	Y	O	C	K	R	D	D	O	M	D	C
I	I	Z	S	A	F	O	K	R	B	H	A	Y	E	A	S	J	L
L	V	N	A	F	X	O	B	A	W	K	P	R	R	S	J	M	N
L	Q	U	C	F	E	K	W	L	Q	W	P	R	U	J	I	L	H
I	Z	Z	T	U	U	S	A	R	M	Y	T	D	C	Y	L	V	V
W	M	C	F	B	H	U	V	O	E	R	Q	E	Q	I	R	X	O
A	M	E	R	I	C	A	N	I	N	D	I	A	N	W	A	R	H

Find These Words

WALKOFHONOR SOLDIER USARMY

SEAMSTRESS WILLIAMCATHAY CONTRABAND

AMERICANINDIANWAR INFANTRYREGIMENT COOK

BUFFALOSOLDIER

If you could meet a cartoon character in real life, who would you pick?

What's your favorite thing about the Army?

What is one thing you want to know about the military?

Directions: Read and answer the questions below. There are clues in the puzzle to help you. Try and solve the cryptic message.

Clue for cryptic message: Cathay is the only female to be this in the 1800's.

Questions

1) Cathay is the only documented woman to _____ in the U. S. Army posing as a man during the American Indian Wars.

2) Cathay was the only known female ____ Soldier.

3) Cathay went by the pseudonym _____ Cathay while serving her enlistment.

4) Cathay joined the military to make her own living and not be _____ to relatives or friends.

5) Cathay has a monument bench on the Walk of Honor at the National ____ Museum.

6) Cathay wore the _____ uniform during her enlistment.

7) Cathay was the first Black woman to enlist in the U.S. ____.

Directions: This is the WGLT Challenge. Solve the cryptogram. As the puzzle solver, you need to find which number belongs to which character. And this can be pretty challenging! You will need to match the number with the letter. There are some letters given to you below. This will help you solve the other words and unlock more characters. **Good Luck.**

Alexander Augusta

Alexander Augusta

March 8, 1825 – December 21, 1890
SURGEON

99

LEFT BLANK ON PURPOSE

Alexander Augusta

Alexander Augusta

Alexander Augusta

Alexander Augusta

Alexander Augusta

Alexander Augusta

Directions: read the bio below and answer the following questions.

Hi, my name is Alexander Augusta. I was born on March 8, 1825, in Norfolk, VA. In 1856, I graduated from the Medical College at the University of Toronto with a degree in medicine. I was appointed the head of the Toronto City Hospital and was also in charge of an industrial school. In 1863, I was commissioned as a major in the Union Army and appointed as the head surgeon in the 7th U.S. Colored Infantry. I was the United States Army's first African-American physician and the first Black hospital administrator in U.S. history. In 1865, I was promoted to the rank of lieutenant colonel. In 1866, I left the service and at the time, I was the highest-ranking Black officer in the U.S. military. In 1868, I was the first African American to be appointed to the faculty of Howard University and the first to be appointed to any medical college in the United States. I was also the first Black professor of medicine (Howard University in Washington, D.C.).

1. What college did I get my doctrine degree from?
   A. University of Pennsylvania
   B. University of Toronto
   C. University of Virginia
2. What year did I get my commission in the Army?
   A. 1863
   B. 1865
   C. 1866
3. I was the first African American to do what in the U.S.?
   A. Hospital Administrator
   B. Join the Army
   C. Lead an Infantry Unit

Directions: Answer the questions, to solve the crossword puzzle. You can use the internet if you get stuck on any question.

Across

3) Alexander was a surgeon in the American _____.

6) Alexander was at the rank of brevet lieutenant _____ in the U.S. Army

7) Alexander was the United States Army's first African-American _____ and its highest-ranking African-American officer at the time.

8) Alexander was the first African American to be appointed to the faculty at any ____ in the United States.

Down

1) Alexander taught _____ in the recently organized medical department at Howard University.

2) Alexander was the first black professor of ____ in the United States.

4) Alexander established a _____ practice in Toronto, Canada West.

5) Alexander was the first African American to be appointed to the faculty of ____ University.

Directions: Read and answer the questions. These are your opinions so the answers will vary.

When was the United States Army established?

What is the largest branch of the United States military?

Which branch of the military is responsible for naval warfare?

Directions: Unscramble the words below about Alexander. See if you can get the bonus word.

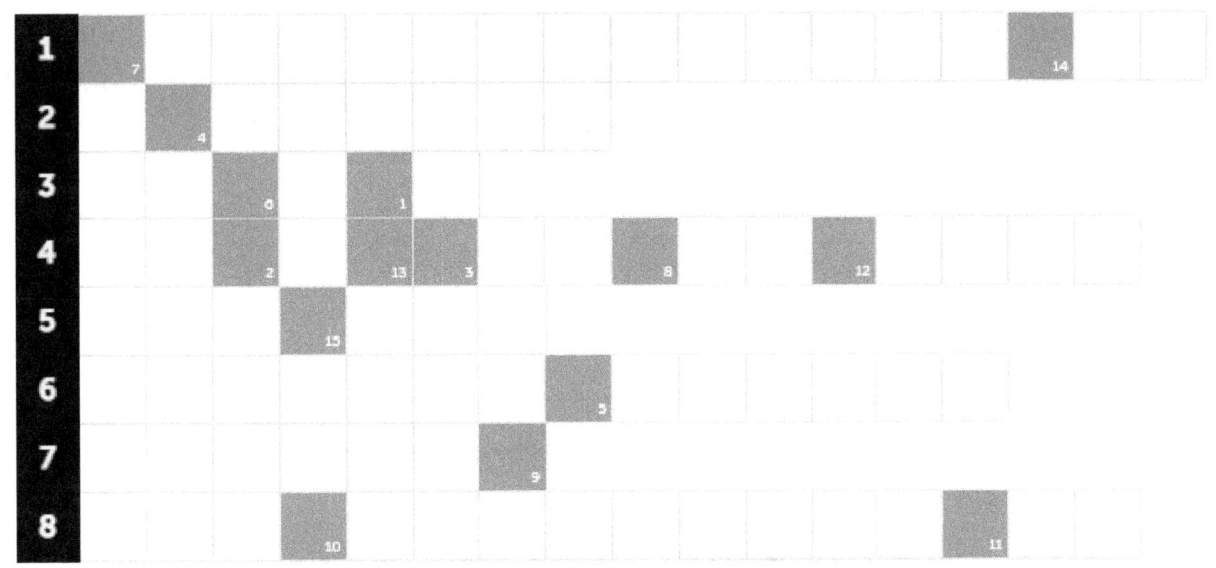

BONUS WORD

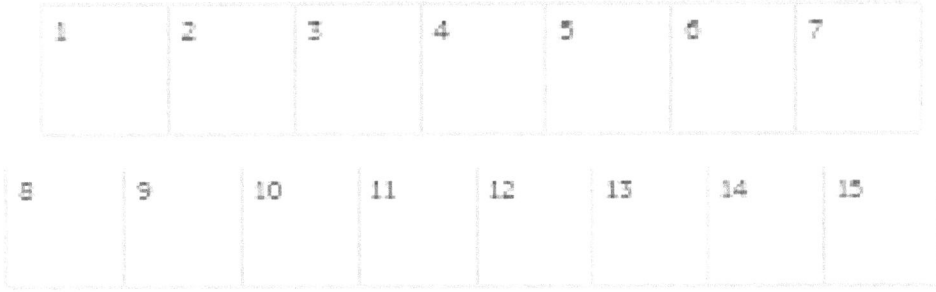

Unscramble Words

1) neanonleucotlitle
2) airwvcli
3) uyrsam
4) nenlnitolipdcesr
5) orgusne
6) titlyiclonrege
7) eofcrfi
8) nsrywiauheoivrdt

Directions: This is the WGLT Challenge. Solve the cryptogram. As the puzzle solver, you need to find which number belongs to which character. And this can be pretty challenging! You will need to match the number with the letter. There are some letters given to you below. This will help you solve the other words and unlock more characters. **Good Luck.**

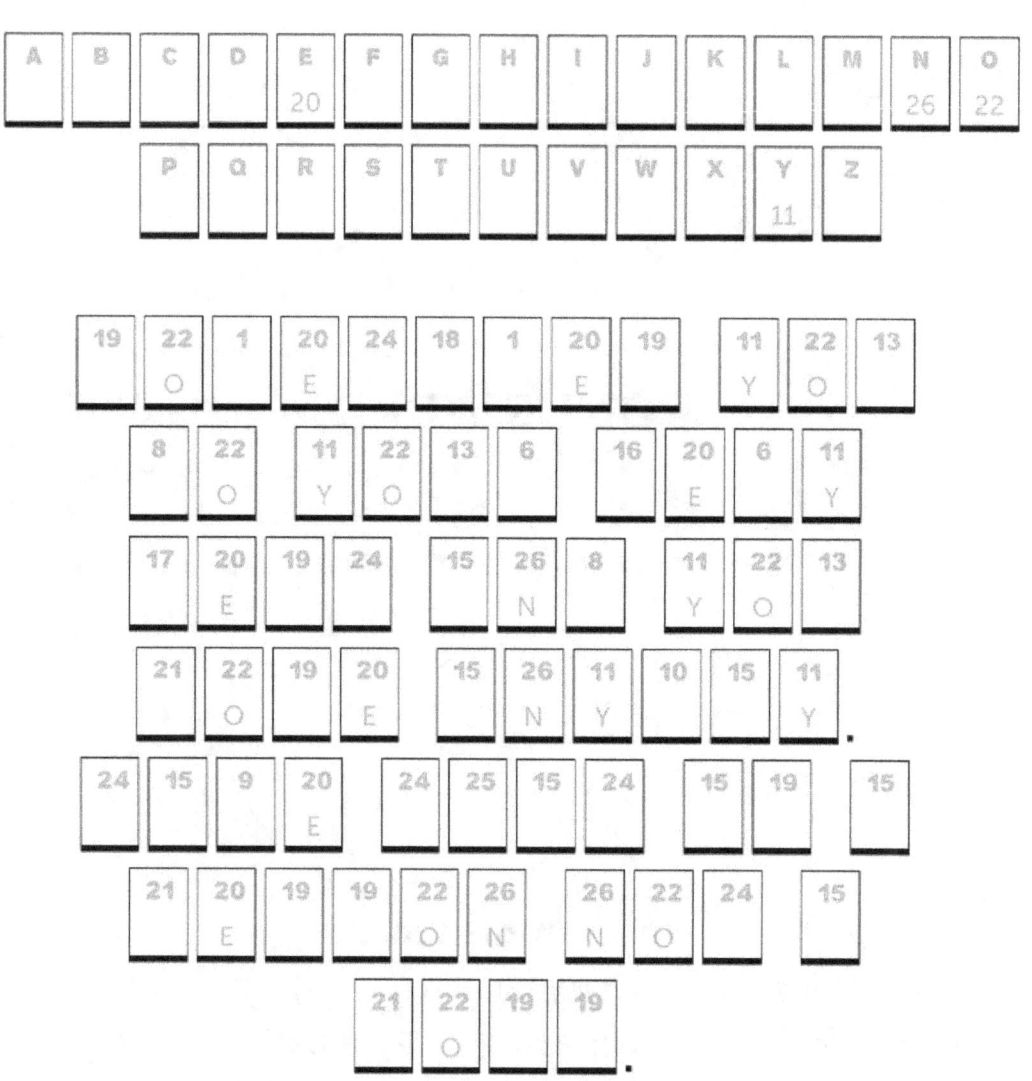

Harriet Pickens

Harriet Pickens

Frances Wills

Frances Wills

March 17, 1909 - 1969
OFFICER

July 12, 1910 - January 18, 1998
OFFICER

107

LEFT BLANK ON PURPOSE

Harriet Pickens

Harriet Pickens

Harriet Pickens

Harriet Pickens

Harriet Pickens

Harriet Pickens

Frances Wills

Frances Wills

Frances Wills

Frances Wills

Frances Wills

Frances Wills

Directions: read the bio below and answer the following questions.

Hi, my name is Harriet Pickens. I was born on March 17, 1909, in Talladega, AL. I graduated from Wadleigh High School. I graduated cum laude from Smith College. I got my master's degree in political science from Columbia University. In 1944, the U.S. Navy opened the WAVES (Women Accepted for Volunteer Emergency Service) program for officer candidacy to African American women. They kept me and Frances Wills out for the first three weeks of training, thinking we'd fall behind and never catch up. I caught up during my first week there. I finished third in my class. In 1944, Ensign Wills and I became the first female African American officers in the Navy. I was assigned to the physical training program and led training sessions for WAVES recruits. I was stationed at Hunter College in NY for most of my service but traveled across the country with Ensign Wills to recruit. When the war ended in August 1945, I transferred to the Reserve. I was later honorably discharged as a lieutenant.

1. What college did I get my Masters Degree from?
   A. Smith College
   B. Columbia University
   C. Hunter College
2. What was my rank in the Navy?
   A. Lieutenant
   B. Ensign
   C. Major
3. We was the first African American women to do what?
   A. Become Enlisted in the Navy
   B. Recruit for the Navy
   C. Become Officers in the Navy

Directions: read the bio below and answer the following questions.

Hi my name is Frances Wills. I was born on July 12, 1910, in Philadelphia, PA. I graduated from George Washington High School. I attended Hunter College and received a Master of Social Work degree from the University of Pittsburgh. I worked at an adoption agency, where I managed the care of children in adoptive homes and the YMCA where I organized community events and social aid. In 1944, the US Navy opened the WAVES (Women Accepted for Volunteer Emergency Service) program for officer candidacy to African American women. I volunteered for the U.S. Navy in November of 1944 and attended the Naval Reserve Midshipmen's School at Smith College. In December of 1944, Lieutenant Pickens and I became the first female African American officers in the Navy. I was assigned to Hunter College, where I taught Naval History and worked as the classification test administrator for enlisted WAVES. In 1945, I went to work as a secretary for Langston Hughes.

1. What was my Masters Degree in?
   A. Medical
   B. Mathematics
   C. Social Work
2. What college was I assigned to?
   A. Smith College
   B. Columbia University
   C. Hunter College
3. What did I work as, at the college?
   A. Naval History
   B. Classification test administrator
   C. English

Directions: Find the words associated with Pickens and Wills' life and career.

C	O	L	U	M	B	I	A	U	N	I	V	E	R	S	I	T	Y
K	V	U	T	G	Q	J	I	Q	X	R	E	S	H	B	P	E	L
C	F	J	M	Y	L	O	M	Q	F	I	Z	N	E	F	T	N	E
A	Q	L	F	V	I	L	J	K	S	E	V	A	W	Z	L	S	D
P	M	J	A	Y	E	U	R	L	A	M	W	K	Z	O	R	I	G
T	G	H	E	P	U	H	J	C	A	K	A	L	L	W	H	G	W
A	E	G	L	P	T	U	G	I	T	A	C	U	L	Z	D	N	S
I	P	U	W	C	E	W	O	R	L	D	W	A	R	T	W	O	I
N	O	V	C	S	N	E	G	E	L	L	O	C	H	T	I	M	S
M	Q	M	M	W	A	E	U	U	C	P	L	J	N	P	D	S	G
C	B	H	C	M	N	Y	U	V	F	P	D	I	W	K	X	Y	L
A	U	V	P	D	T	X	V	B	Z	H	D	B	F	G	O	T	D
F	U	H	B	W	V	X	X	A	V	G	S	V	L	Z	L	X	B
E	R	T	T	E	H	O	J	E	N	O	V	Z	N	Y	W	C	A
E	K	Z	H	U	X	U	R	A	I	S	X	V	S	K	X	B	W
Q	T	Z	L	O	K	A	S	G	T	G	U	W	T	X	I	Q	Y
S	F	E	F	W	R	I	N	A	A	C	P	J	M	Z	Z	Q	M
C	V	T	P	B	W	W	K	Q	T	D	E	F	H	X	S	Q	N

Find These Words

WAVES	LIEUTENANT	ENSIGN
AUTHOR	COLUMBIAUNIVERSITY	NAACP
SMITHCOLLEGE	CAPTAINMCAFEE	WORLDWARTWO
USNAVY		

Directions: This is the WGLT Challenge. Solve the cryptogram. As the puzzle solver, you need to find which number belongs to which character. And this can be pretty challenging! You will need to match the number with the letter. There are some letters given to you below. This will help you solve the other words and unlock more characters. **Good Luck.**

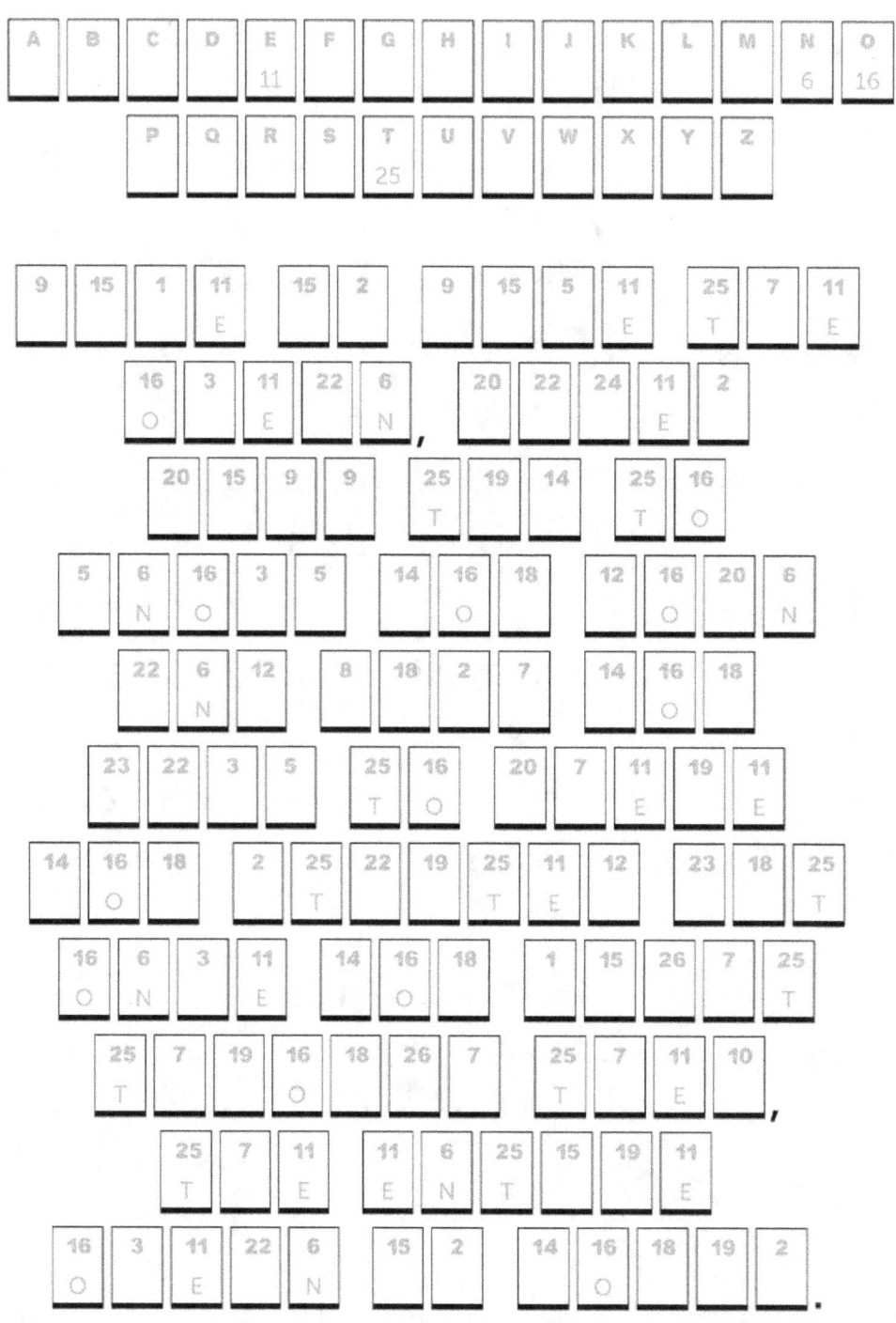

Frank Petersen Jr.

Frank Petersen Jr.

March 2, 1932 – August 25, 2015
OFFICER

115

LEFT BLANK ON PURPOSE

Frank Petersen Jr.

Frank Petersen Jr.

Frank Petersen Jr.

Frank Petersen Jr.

Frank Petersen Jr.

Frank Petersen Jr.

Hi, my name is Frank Petersen Jr. I was born on March 2, 1932, in Topeka, KS. I graduated from Topeka High School. I got my Bachelor of Arts degree and my master's degree in international affairs from George Washington University. I also graduated from the National War College. I joined the United States Navy as a seaman apprentice and served as an electronic technician. In 1950, I entered the Naval Aviation Cadet Program and in 1952, after finishing flight training, I became the first Black Marine aviator. I was commissioned as a second lieutenant in the United States Marine Corps (USMC). My first tactical assignment was with VMFA-212 during the Korean War. I flew over 350 combat missions and worked over 4,000 hours in various fighter/attack aircraft. I became the first African American to command a squadron: the Marine Fighter Attack Squadron 314 (VMFA-314), which was also known as the Black Knights, in Vietnam. In 1979, I was promoted to brigadier general, which made me the first African American general in USMC history.

1. What college did I get my Master Degree from?
   A. Kansas University
   B. New York University
   C. George Washington University
2. I became the first African American General in?
   A. USMC
   B. USN
   C. USAF
3. I was the first black Marine _____?
   A. Grunt
   B. Technician
   C. Aviator

Directions: Answer the questions, to solve the crossword puzzle. You can use the internet if you get stuck on any question.

Across

4) Frank flew over 290 combat missions during ___ War.

6) Frank flew 64 combat missions during the ____ War.

7) Frank was also awarded the ____ because he was wounded in action.

8) Frank was appointed to the Board of Visitors to the United States _____ by President Obama.

Down

1) Frank was awarded the ___ Eagle Trophy in 1988.

2) Frank was the first African-American Marine Corps ____.

3) Frank was the first African-American Marine Corps ____.

5) Frank flew an F-4 _____ in the Marine Corps.

Directions: Read and answer the questions. These are your opinions so the answers will vary.

What is the primary role of the United States Navy?

Which branch of the military is responsible for maintaining control of the skies?

What is the main function of the United States Air Force?

Directions: Unscramble the words below about Frank. See if you can get the bonus word.

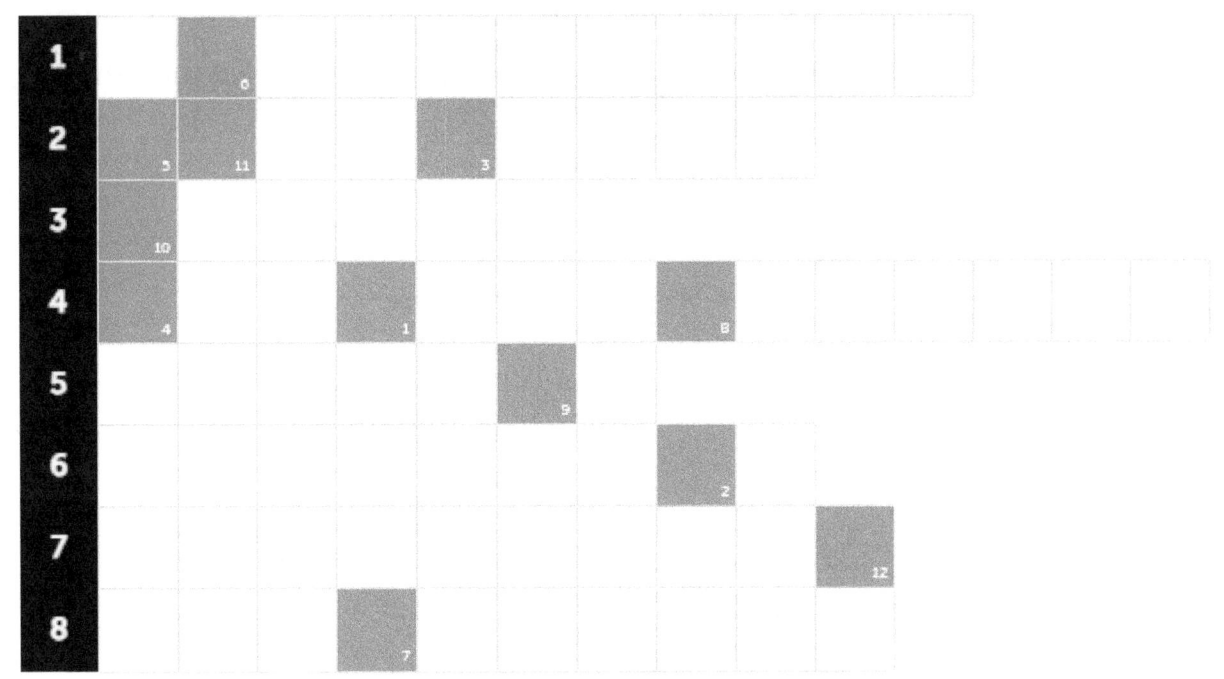

BONUS WORD

1	2	3	4	5	6	7	8	9	10	11	12

Unscramble Words

1) rrpseomnica **2)** erakwrnoa **3)** kapteo

4) siotibssocamnm **5)** eglaenr **6)** gaaeylreg

7) rwtavenaim **8)** shrikwlvae

Directions: This is the WGLT Challenge. Solve the cryptogram. As the puzzle solver, you need to find which number belongs to which character. And this can be pretty challenging! You will need to match the number with the letter. There are some letters given to you below. This will help you solve the other words and unlock more characters. **Good Luck.**

Michael Langley

Michael Langley

March 2, 1961 – PRESENT
OFFICER

LEFT BLANK ON PURPOSE

Michael Langley

Michael Langley

Michael Langley

Michael Langley

Michael Langley

Michael Langley

Directions: read the bio below and answer the following questions.

Hi my name is **Michael Langley**. I was born in 1960, in Shreveport, LA. I graduated from the University of Texas at Arlington and commissioned as a Second Lieutenant in 1985. While at University of Texas I became a member of Kappa Alpha Psi Fraternity. Here are some of the platoons and regiments I've commanded. Battery K, 5th Battalion, 11th Marines in support of Operations WILDFIRE in Western United States; battalion and regimental commands in 12th Marines forward deployed in Okinawa, Japan; and both the 201st Regional Corps Advisory Command-Central and Regional Support Command – Southwest in support of Operation ENDURING FREEDOM in Afghanistan. As a General Officer, here are some of my command assignments, include Deputy Commanding General, II Marine Expeditionary Force (MEF) and Commanding General, 2d Marine Expeditionary Brigade; Commander, Marine Forces Europe and Africa. I'm the first black four-star general in the 246-year history of the Marine Corps.

1. What college did I get my Bachelors Degree from?
   A. Kansas University
   B. University of Texas
   C. George Washington University
2. I became the first African American four-star General in?
   A. USMC
   B. USN
   C. USAF
3. Which regiment didn't I command?
   A. II Marine Expeditionary Force
   B. Marine Forces Europe
   C. U.S. 5th Fleet

Directions: Find the words associated with Michael's life and career.

C	U	U	T	D	A	R	S	E	T	U	Y	P	I	W	X	G	B
E	N	G	V	V	A	H	D	R	U	I	B	B	L	F	W	I	M
Y	I	S	B	R	L	O	U	I	S	I	A	N	A	M	N	B	E
Y	V	J	R	A	W	N	A	T	S	I	N	A	H	G	F	A	C
N	E	N	E	E	M	B	X	J	I	R	P	Y	C	Y	I	C	R
P	R	G	G	S	Z	Z	R	O	P	X	D	O	D	S	G	L	O
H	S	M	L	D	P	E	U	O	E	W	S	S	A	Q	V	J	F
A	I	S	L	E	G	R	P	S	N	C	C	T	Y	A	O	I	E
B	T	S	Y	M	O	U	O	O	A	Z	M	I	H	S	W	J	N
E	Y	M	E	W	Q	B	D	C	R	X	E	S	B	J	O	W	I
K	O	V	G	M	Y	K	J	J	E	U	L	S	C	U	H	D	R
R	F	C	Y	A	P	T	O	S	S	N	E	O	T	T	X	M	A
V	T	A	B	D	H	E	R	G	E	V	I	Z	Z	A	H	B	M
Z	E	T	W	K	B	B	R	F	C	M	M	R	T	F	R	R	T
K	X	H	W	G	P	U	P	F	D	V	Z	Q	A	O	P	R	E
F	A	H	B	C	P	D	E	P	I	B	T	Q	Q	M	T	R	E
R	S	F	O	U	R	S	T	A	R	G	E	N	E	R	A	L	L
F	Y	Q	S	H	A	R	P	S	H	O	O	T	E	R	H	U	F

Find These Words

SEMPERFI	SHARPSHOOTER	BRONZESTAR
FOURSTARGENERAL	UNIVERSITYOFTEXAS	AFGHANISTANWAR
MARINECORPS	EUROPE	LOUISIANA
FLEETMARINEFORCE		

Directions: Read and answer the questions. These are your opinions so the answers will vary.

What is the primary mission of the United States Marine Corps?

Which branch of the military specializes in amphibious operations?

What is the main function of the United States Space Force?

Directions: Read and answer the questions below. There are clues in the puzzle to help you. Try and solve the cryptic message.

Clue for cryptic message: Michael will always be this.

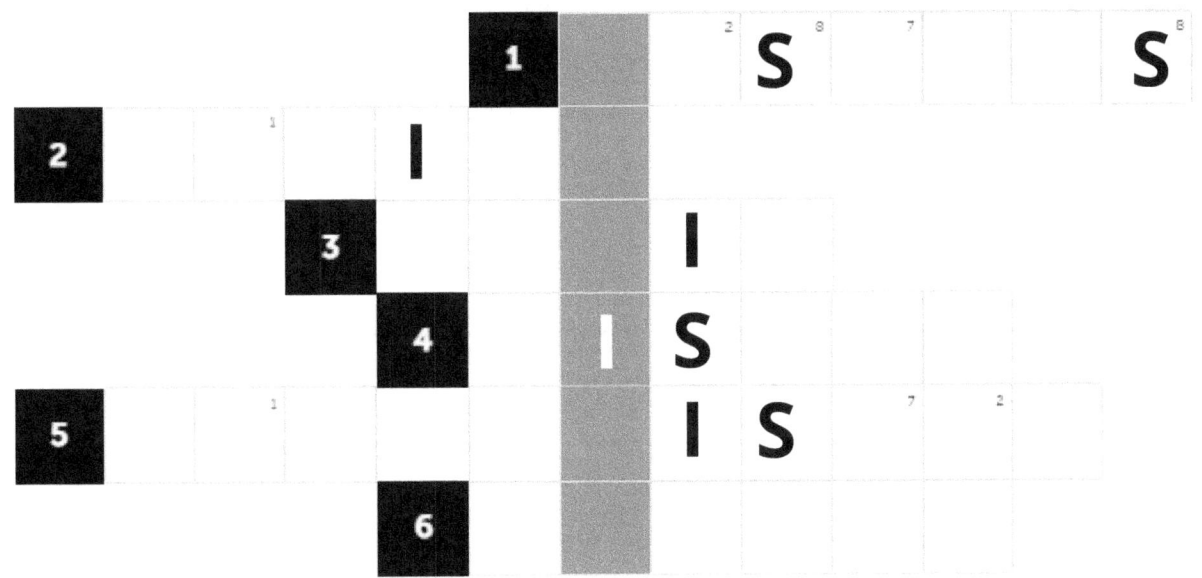

Questions

1) Michael got his ____ degree in strategic studies from the United States Army War College.

2) Michael was the commander of United States Marine Forces ____.

3) Michael was awarded the Legion of ____ award twice for exceptionally meritorious conduct.

4) Michael was a sharpshooter with the rifle and the ____.

5) Michael served in the ____ War.

6) Michael served as ____ commander of Fleet Marine Force, Atlantic.

Directions: This is the WGLT Challenge. Solve the cryptogram. As the puzzle solver, you need to find which number belongs to which character. And this can be pretty challenging! You will need to match the number with the letter. There are some letters given to you below. This will help you solve the other words and unlock more characters. **Good Luck.**

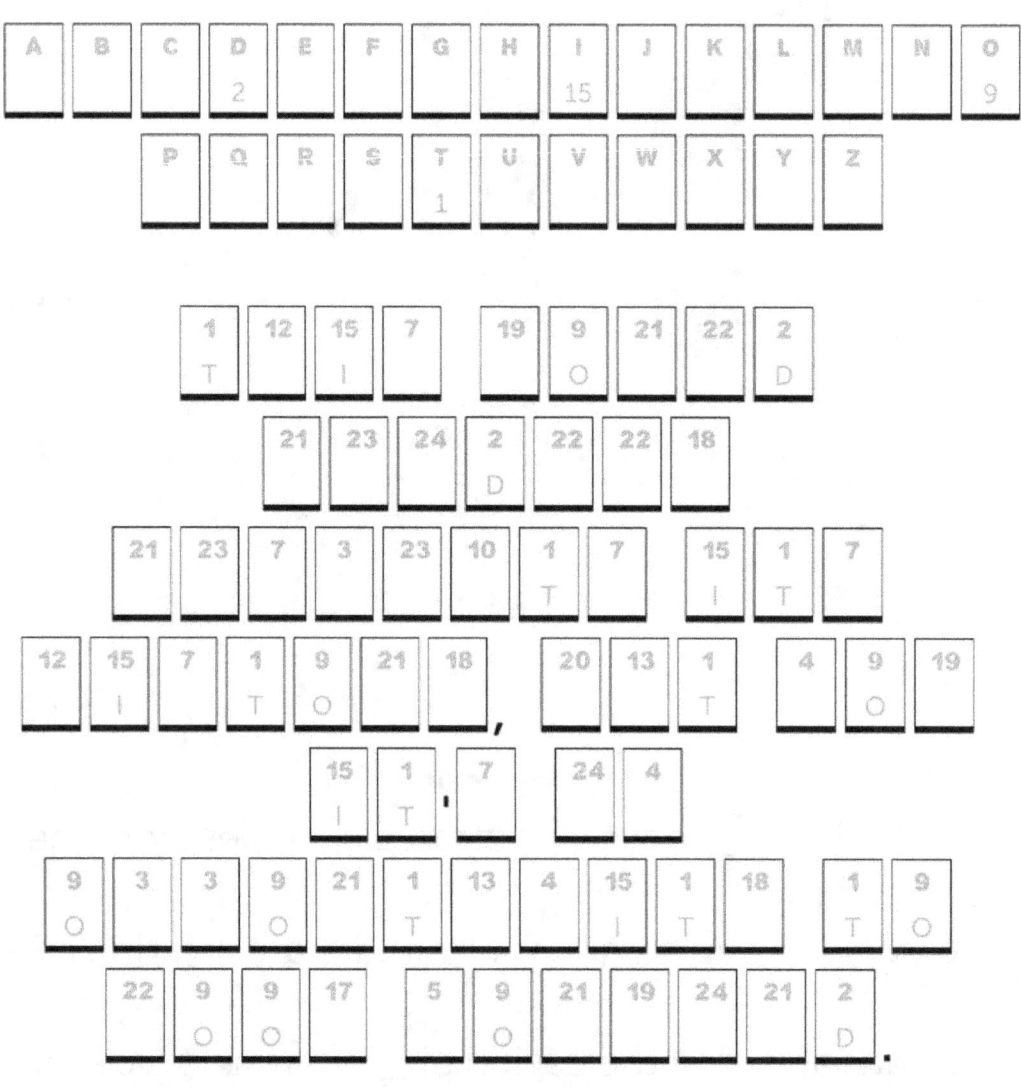

Charles Brown Jr.

Charles Brown Jr.

1962 - PRESENT
OFFICER

131

LEFT BLANK ON PURPOSE

Charles Brown Jr.

Charles Brown Jr.

Charles Brown Jr.

Charles Brown Jr.

Charles Brown Jr.

Charles Brown Jr.

Directions: read the bio below and answer the following questions.

Hi, my name is Charles Brown Jr. I was born in 1962 in Lubbock, TX. I graduated from the Air Force Reserve Officers Training Corps at Texas Tech University with a Bachelor of Science in Civil Engineering. I became a member of the Alpha Phi Alpha fraternity. I received my master's degree in aeronautical science from Embry-Riddle Aeronautical University. In 1985, I was commissioned as a second lieutenant after completing the Air Force Reserve Officers Training Corps program in the United States Air Force (USAF). Some of my assignments as a commander were with the Pacific Air Forces (PACAF), United States Indo-Pacific Command (USINDOPACOM) and United States Central Command (CENTCOM). In 2020, I was unanimously confirmed as Chief of Staff of the U.S. Air Force. With this appointment, I became the first African American to lead a branch of the United States Armed Forces. As Air Force Chief of Staff, I advise the president, secretary of defense and National Security Council regarding Air Force matters.

1. What fraternity am I a member of?
   A. Omega Psi Phi
   B. Alpha Phi Alpha
   C. Phi Beta Sigma
2. What year did I did I get my commission with the USAF?
   A. 1989
   B. 1985
   C. 1983
3. I was the first African American to lead what?
   A. A branch of the United States Armed Forces
   B. A military University
   C. A military squadron

Directions: Answer the questions, to solve the crossword puzzle. You can use the internet if you get stuck on any question.

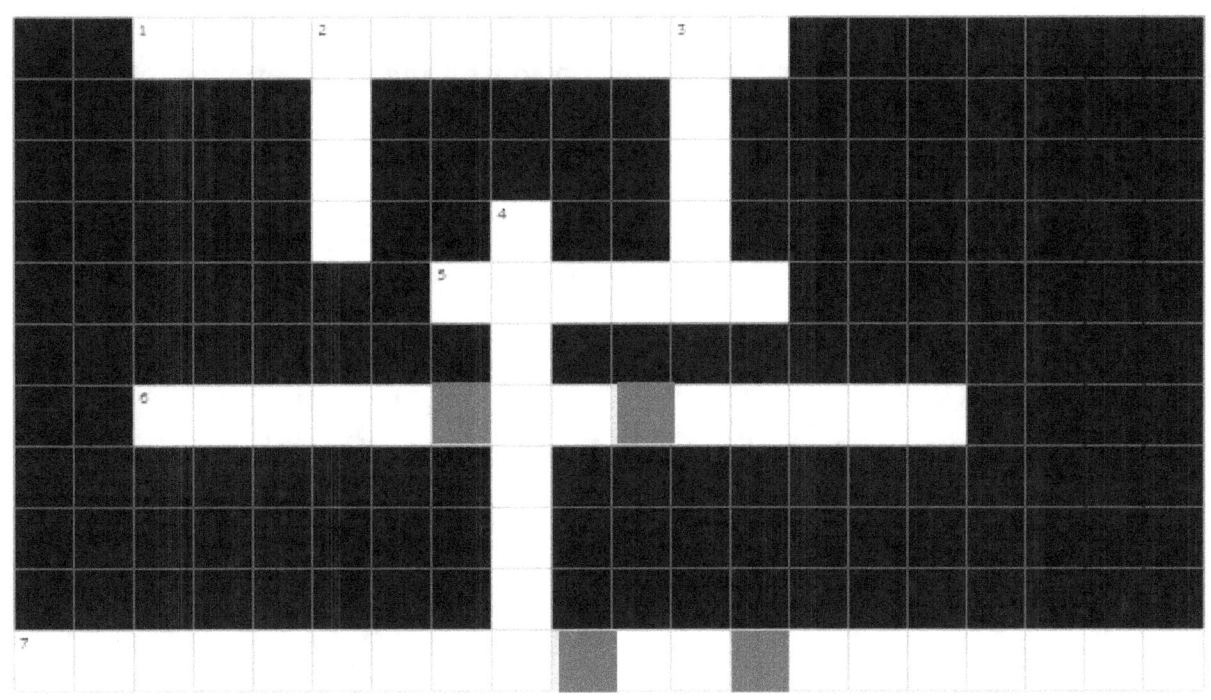

Across

1) Charles was named by Time magazine on its list of the 100 most ____ people in the world.

5) Charles has around 130 ____ hours.

6) Charles was the first African American to be appointed as ____.

7) Charles was the first African American to serve as a United States ____.

Down

2) Charles was the first African American to ____ any branch of the United States Armed Forces.

3) Charles is a member of ____ Phi Alpha fraternity.

4) Charles was made an ____ Tuskegee Airman.

Directions: Read and answer the questions. These are your opinions so the answers will vary.

Which branch of the military focuses on providing medical services to personnel?

What is the primary mission of the United States Coast Guard?

Which branch of the military operates submarines?

Directions: Unscramble the words below about Charles. See if you can get the bonus word.

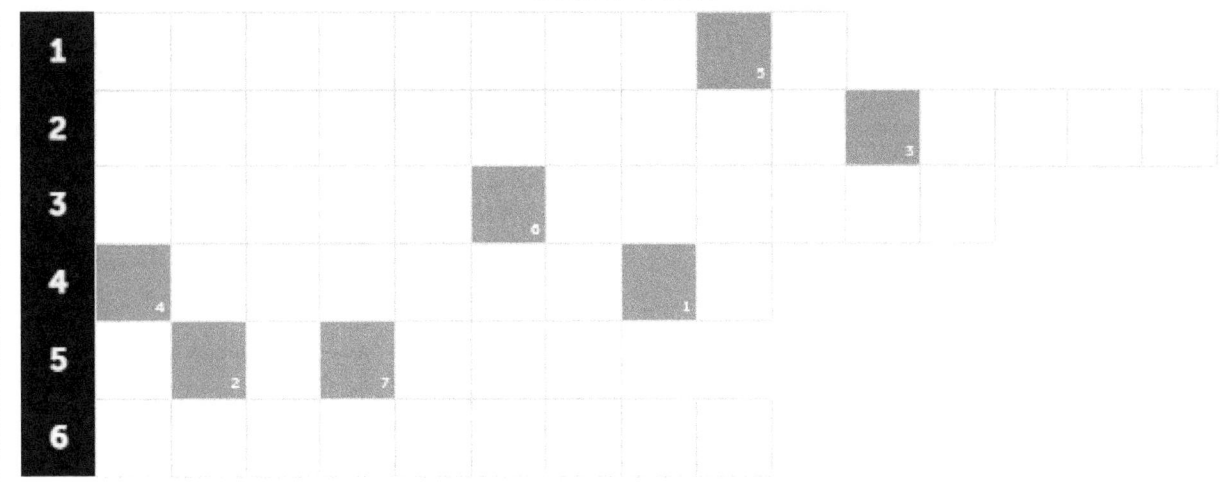

BONUS WORD

1	2	3	4	5	6	7

Unscramble Words

1) sruaioecfr   **2)** eersonauafrgrtl   **3)** ffsfcfoaieth

4) ettcshxea   **5)** eargnym   **6)** iasoidnen

Directions: This is the WGLT Challenge. Solve the cryptogram. As the puzzle solver, you need to find which number belongs to which character. And this can be pretty challenging! You will need to match the number with the letter. There are some letters given to you below. This will help you solve the other words and unlock more characters. **Good Luck.**

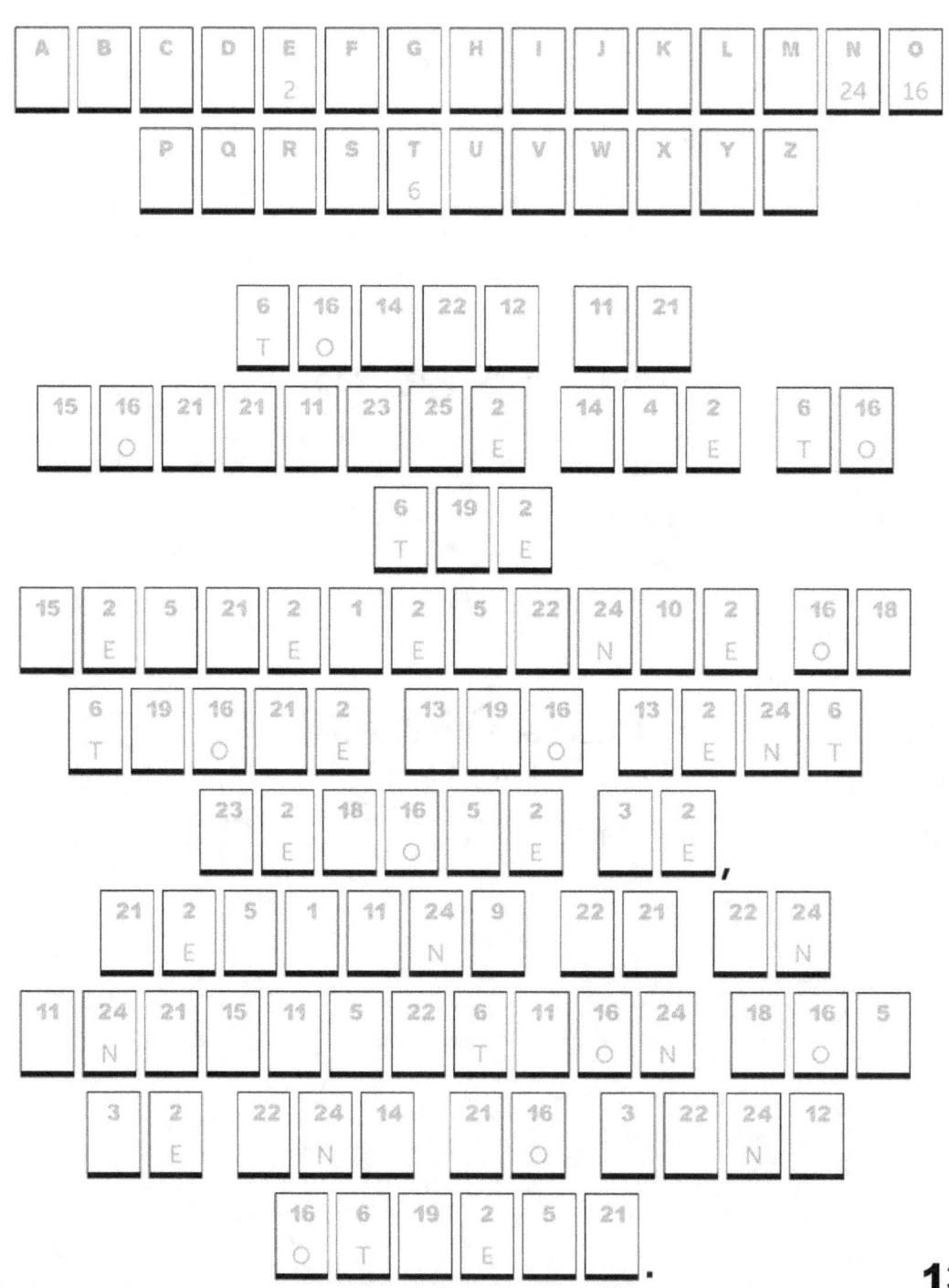

Michelle Howard

Michelle Howard

April 30, 1960 - PRESENT
OFFICER

LEFT BLANK ON PURPOSE

Michelle Howard

Michelle Howard

Michelle Howard

Michelle Howard

Michelle Howard

Michelle Howard

Directions: read the bio below and answer the following questions.

Hi, my name is Michelle Howard. I was born on April 30, 1960, at March Air Force Base in CA. I graduated from Gateway High School. I got a Bachelor of Science from the United States Naval Academy. I received my Master of Military Art and Science from the United States Army Command and General Staff College. In 1999, I assumed command of the USS Rushmore and became the first African American woman to command a ship in the United States Navy. In 2006, I was promoted to the rank of rear admiral (lower half). I was the first admiral who was selected from the United States Naval Academy class of 1982 and the first female graduate of the United States Naval Academy who was selected for a flag rank. In 2014, I was appointed vice chief of naval operations, which made me the second-highest-ranking officer in the Navy. I also became the first female four-star admiral to command operational forces after I assumed command of the United States Naval Forces in Europe and the Naval Forces in Africa. I'm the highest-ranking woman in United States Naval history.

1. What was the name of the ship I first took command of?
   A. USS Hunley
   B. USS Rushmore
   C. USS Lexington

2. What year did I become a four star admiral?
   A. 2014
   B. 2012
   C. 2010

3. I'm the highest-ranking woman in what branch?
   A. United States Marine Corps history
   B. United States Army history
   C. United States Naval history

Directions: Find the words associated with Michelle's life and career.

K	F	S	U	Y	I	W	S	C	Q	T	P	Q	Z	M	Y	X	P
U	K	P	S	A	W	S	S	U	H	A	C	J	F	N	E	G	Q
S	W	J	N	A	V	A	L	A	C	A	D	E	M	Y	U	Z	S
S	N	N	J	C	F	K	G	Z	N	B	L	P	F	O	S	N	L
M	H	B	Y	G	L	V	A	U	Y	J	F	D	T	G	S	O	D
O	W	H	O	L	K	S	Q	E	L	I	G	U	P	F	R	O	E
U	K	M	M	P	W	G	L	W	T	F	X	S	E	M	U	T	S
N	J	Y	Z	W	L	N	D	R	Z	E	W	I	R	F	S	L	E
T	A	M	V	I	U	U	H	I	Z	N	I	A	K	N	H	B	R
H	L	I	G	H	W	V	S	B	S	N	M	X	R	Y	M	K	T
O	Z	Z	S	R	Y	V	A	N	S	U	R	Q	Y	X	O	R	S
O	Y	S	T	A	M	T	P	H	O	C	Z	U	M	T	R	M	T
D	U	P	K	F	W	I	Z	D	N	D	M	F	I	E	E	X	O
L	Y	P	O	Z	S	W	F	Z	L	A	R	I	M	D	A	A	R
N	Z	V	M	C	P	N	R	J	L	N	E	Y	R	S	P	W	M
P	I	O	X	K	Q	C	X	M	R	V	H	T	J	J	X	Q	U
Y	V	S	P	H	W	W	D	G	R	V	Z	Z	T	U	P	D	B
K	C	U	S	S	L	E	X	I	N	G	T	O	N	J	F	V	S

Find These Words

USNAVY   USSRUSHMORE   ADMIRAL
USSHUNLEY   GULFWAR   USSWASP
NAVALACADEMY   USSLEXINGTON   DESERTSTORM
USSMOUNTHOOD

Which branch of the military focuses on strategic missile defense?

What is the primary role of the United States Army Reserve?

What is the main function of the United States National Guard?

Directions: Read and answer the questions below. There are clues in the puzzle to help you. Try and solve the cryptic message.

Clue for cryptic message: Michelle served on this vessel .

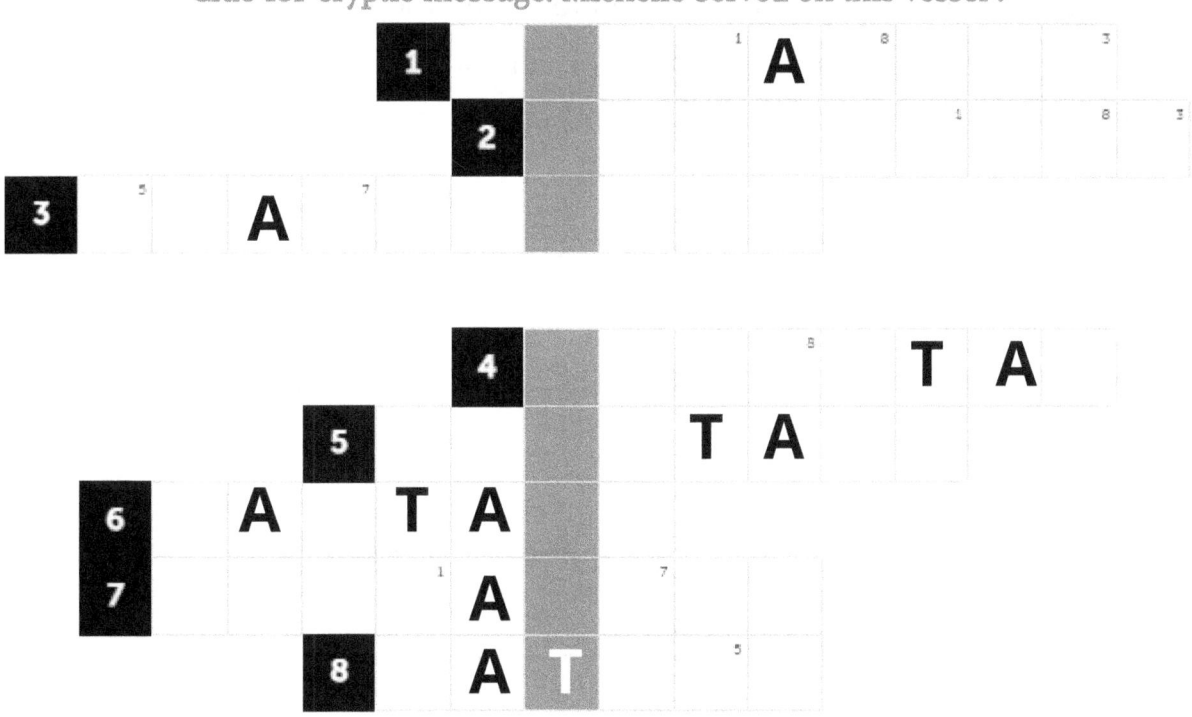

Questions

1) Michelle first sea duty was aboard the _____ tender USS Hunley for three years.

2) Michelle piloted her first ship, the destroyer USS Spruance, during her _____ year at the academy.

3) Michelle earned the Secretary of the Navy/Navy League Captain Winifred Collins Award, given annually to a female officer who exhibited outstanding ____.

4) Michelle was the first woman to become a _____ admiral in the U.S. Navy.

5) Michelle was awarded the USO _____ Woman of the Year in 2011.

6) Michelle was the first African American woman to ___ a U.S. naval ship.

7) Michelle held the post Deputy _____ U.S. Fleet Forces in 2012.

8) Michelle was the first African American woman to lead a U.S. Navy ___ group when she took command of Expeditionary Strike Group Two. **145**

Directions: This is the WGLT Challenge. Solve the cryptogram. As the puzzle solver, you need to find which number belongs to which character. And this can be pretty challenging! You will need to match the number with the letter. There are some letters given to you below. This will help you solve the other words and unlock more characters. **Good Luck.**

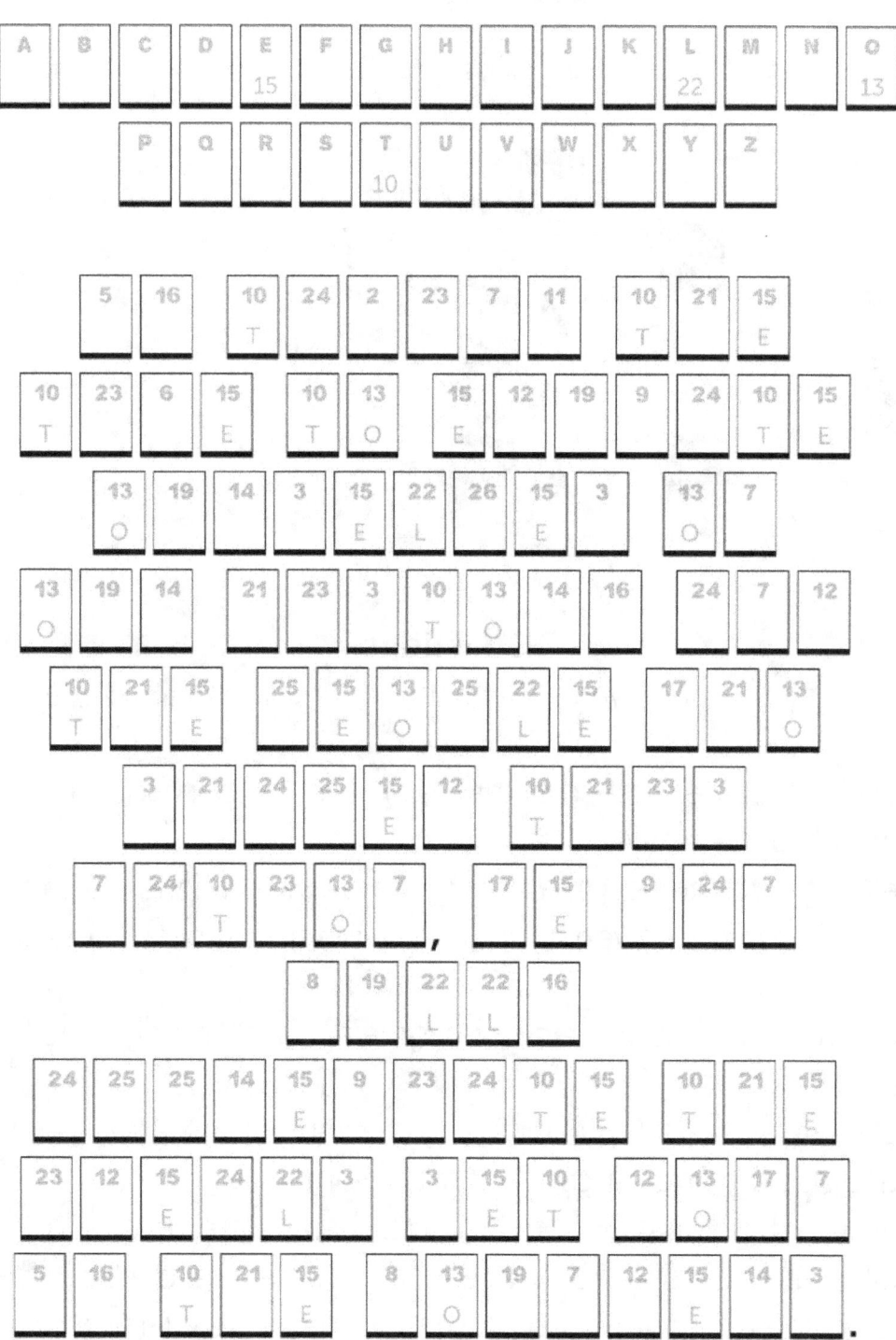

Doris Miller

Doris Miller

October 12, 1919 – November 24, 1943
NAVY COOK

LEFT BLANK ON PURPOSE

Doris Miller

Doris Miller

Doris Miller

Doris Miller

Doris Miller

Doris Miller

Hi, my name is Doris Miller. I was born on October 12, 1919, in Waco, TX. I attended Alexander James Moore High School. In 1939, I joined the Navy and after completing boot camp training, I was assigned to the USS West Virginia as a mess attendant, which was one of the only occupational specialties that was open to Black men at that time. On December 7, 1941, aboard the West Virginia The Japanese aircraft carrier Akagi fired the first of seven torpedoes that hit the West Virginia. I was ordered to the bridge to help the skipper, who was wounded. While there, I was ordered to help load the unmanned Browning .50 caliber anti-aircraft machine guns. I was not familiar with the weapon, but they instructed me on how to operate it. I fired the gun and hit a few planes. After the Pittsburgh Courier and the NAACP put some pressure on the Navy, I became the first Black American to be awarded the Navy Cross, which is the highest decoration for valor in combat after the Medal of Honor.

1. What was the name of the ship I was assigned to first?
   A. USS West Virginia
   B. USS Nevada
   C. USS Liscome Bay (CVE-56)
2. What year did Japanese aircraft carrier Akagi attack?
   A. 1939
   B. 1941
   C. 1943
3. I was the first African American to get awarded?
   A. Medal of Honor
   B. Purple Heart
   C. Navy Cross

Directions: Answer the questions, to solve the crossword puzzle. You can use the internet if you get stuck on any question.

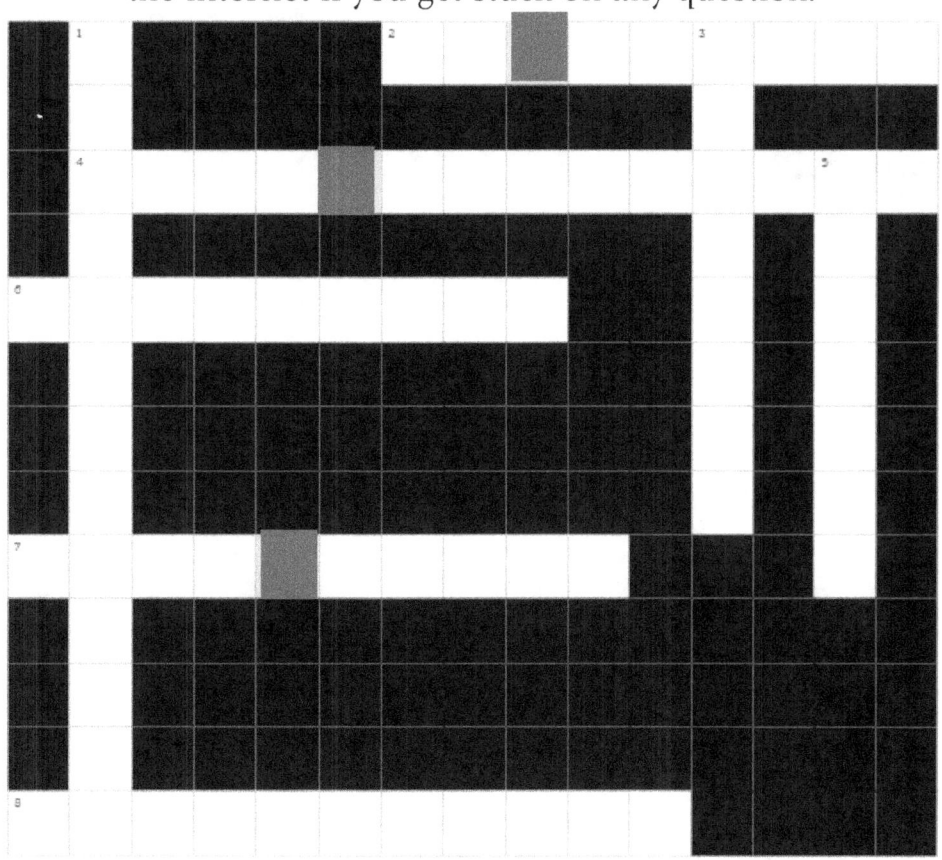

Across

2) Doris was recognized as one of the "first _____ of World War II".

4) Doris was a _____ because that was one of the few ratings open at the time to black sailors.

6) Doris had the _____ escort/Knox-class frigate USS Miller (reclassified as a frigate in June 1975), in service from 1973 to 1991, named after him.

7) Doris was the first Black American to be awarded the _____, the highest decoration for valor presented by the US Navy.

8) Doris started competition boxing and became the ship's _____ champion.

Down

1) Doris was honored by the United States Postal Service as one of four Distinguished Sailors, with a 44-cent _____ stamp.

3) Doris actions allowed the Navy to open up jobs such as gunner's mate, _____ and radar operator to Black sailors and eventually started commissioning Black officers.

5) Doris will have a Gerald R. Ford-class ___ powered aircraft carrier, CVN-81, named after him and launched in 2029.

Directions: Read and answer the questions. These are your opinions so the answers will vary.

Which branch of the military is responsible for conducting military intelligence operations?

What is the primary mission of the United States Cyber Command?

Which branch of the military specializes in explosive ordnance disposal?

Directions: Unscramble the words below about Doris. See if you can get the bonus word.

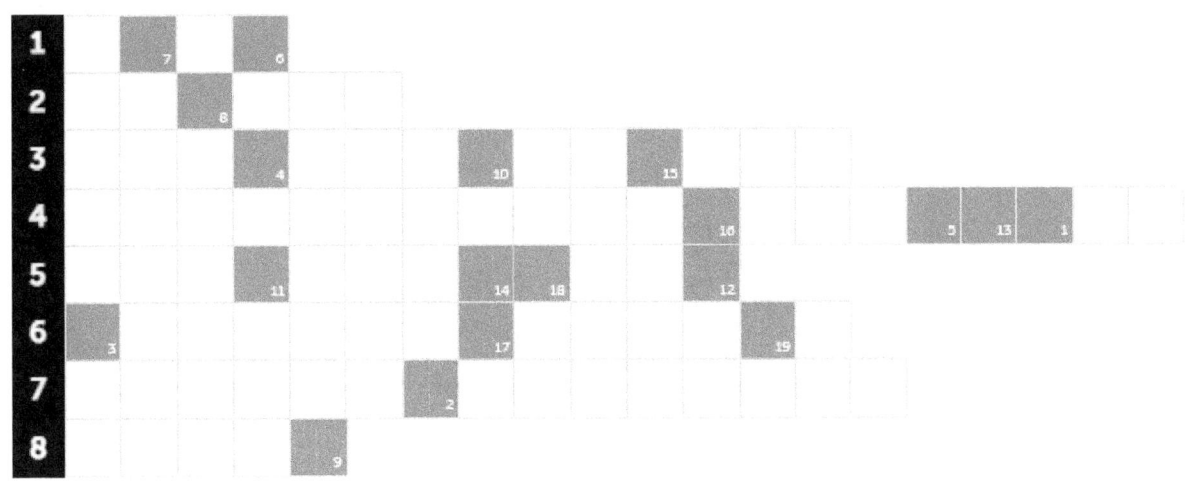

BONUS WORD

Unscramble Words

1) okoc

2) yvusan

3) slsneappaeneaj

4) trdcfltiepy3csefoars

5) fdoralomnhoe

6) rmstpoedboober

7) suesvgiriatniws

8) cpana

Directions: This is the WGLT Challenge. Solve the cryptogram. As the puzzle solver, you need to find which number belongs to which character. And this can be pretty challenging! You will need to match the number with the letter. There are some letters given to you below. This will help you solve the other words and unlock more characters. **Good Luck.**

A	B	C	D	E	F	G	H	I	J	K	L	M	N	O
16							17	1						

P	Q	R	S	T	U	V	W	X	Y	Z
			13							

17	10	11	14	10	13		16	11	10		7	16	25	10
H					S		A					A		

1	2		18	17	10		17	14	9	11		14	22
I				H			H						

25	10	22	10	16	18		13	9	21	21	10	13	13
				A		.	S					S	S

1	13		25	10	13	21	11	1	24	10	25		16	13
I	S				S			I					A	S

16		13	10	11	1	10	13		14	22
A		S			I		S			

19	4	14	11	1	14	9	13
				I			S

25	10	22	10	16	18	13
				A		S |.

154

Hazel Johnson-Brown

Hazel Johnson-Brown

October 10, 1927 – August 5, 2011
OFFICER

155

LEFT BLANK ON PURPOSE

Hazel Johnson-Brown

Hazel Johnson-Brown

Hazel Johnson-Brown

Hazel Johnson-Brown

Hazel Johnson-Brown

Hazel Johnson-Brown

Hi, my name is Hazel Johnson. I was born on October 10, 1927, in West Chester, PA. I graduated from Tredyffrin-Easttown Junior Senior High School. I received my Bachelor of Science in Nursing from Villanova University. I got my Master of Science in Nursing Education from Columbia University. I received my Ph.D. from the Catholic University of America. I joined the Army in 1955. I finished my tour in 1957, so I left, got my bachelor's degree and returned to the Army in 1959. In 1960, I served as the operating room nurse at Walter Reed Army Medical Center. In 1967, I served as the director of the Field Sterilization Equipment Development Project and researched solutions to problems that related to the use of ethylene oxide sterilization. In 1976, I became the director and assistant dean of the Walter Reed Army Institute of Nursing. In 1979, I was nominated to serve as the chief of the Army Nurse Corps. I became the first African American female general in the U.S. Army and the first African American chief of the U.S. Army Nurse Corps.

1. What college did I get my Masters degree from?
   A. Villanova University
   B. Catholic University of America
   C. Columbia University
2. What year did I come back into the Army?
   A. 1959
   B. 1955
   C. 1957
3. In the Army I became the first black female to do what?
   A. Become a head Nurse
   B. Become a General
   C. Become a Doctor

Directions: Find the words associated with Hazel's life and career.

S	B	R	I	G	A	D	I	E	R	G	E	N	E	R	A	L	T
C	E	O	S	D	N	C	X	Y	I	Q	C	F	U	N	A	O	E
Q	D	Q	G	O	J	B	L	O	P	A	Q	L	S	S	R	D	F
I	Z	T	F	R	E	E	O	M	R	M	G	W	A	E	M	R	R
Y	L	R	S	I	M	P	E	I	I	X	F	L	R	Q	Y	O	D
L	P	Z	H	E	K	M	V	F	V	L	N	U	M	E	N	T	U
Z	Y	Q	L	Y	U	E	F	J	Z	V	U	O	Y	A	U	A	P
K	O	R	B	V	Z	G	G	P	X	Z	R	I	B	B	R	C	F
A	A	U	G	E	S	D	W	L	Y	H	S	Q	F	U	S	U	O
H	A	H	W	M	Y	T	C	S	M	E	N	V	S	E	D	Z
W	M	D	E	S	E	R	T	S	T	O	R	M	E	U	C	E	O
J	U	O	H	Q	D	Y	U	G	Y	G	K	L	N	R	O	A	S
L	L	R	E	T	S	E	H	C	T	S	E	W	A	G	R	Q	W
O	O	O	C	X	G	C	K	F	K	Q	Y	W	O	E	P	V	C
B	V	T	T	P	U	L	U	D	R	T	P	G	U	O	S	V	K
R	W	C	D	H	Y	C	T	L	H	X	M	X	A	N	J	K	Z
K	H	Q	C	A	S	L	Z	K	F	U	U	P	F	E	I	H	C
I	D	L	J	Z	K	I	R	Z	W	T	U	S	N	K	I	D

Find These Words

HARLEM   NURSE   USARMY
EDUCATOR   SURGEON   DESERTSTORM
BRIGADIERGENERAL   CHIEF   WESTCHESTER
ARMYNURSECORPS

What is the main function of the United States Military Police Corps?

What are the five branches of the United States military?

What is the oldest branch of the United States military?

Directions: Read and answer the questions below. There are clues in the puzzle to help you. Try and solve the cryptic message.

Clue for cryptic message: Hazel was great as this.

Questions

1) Hazel's nursing career started at the _____ Hospital emergency ward.

2) Hazel earned her _____ in educational administration from Catholic University.

3) Hazel was awarded the Army _____ Service Medal.

4) Hazel was the first Black _____ of the United States Army Nurse Corps.

5) Hazel was the first Black female _____ in the United States Army.

6) Hazel was awarded army nurse of the year _____.

7) Hazel was mentioned in _____ magazine as "one of the real 'heavies' in her field".

8) Hazel was head _____ of the Philadelphia Veteran's Administration Hospital.

Directions: This is the WGLT Challenge. Solve the cryptogram. As the puzzle solver, you need to find which number belongs to which character. And this can be pretty challenging! You will need to match the number with the letter. There are some letters given to you below. This will help you solve the other words and unlock more characters. **Good Luck.**

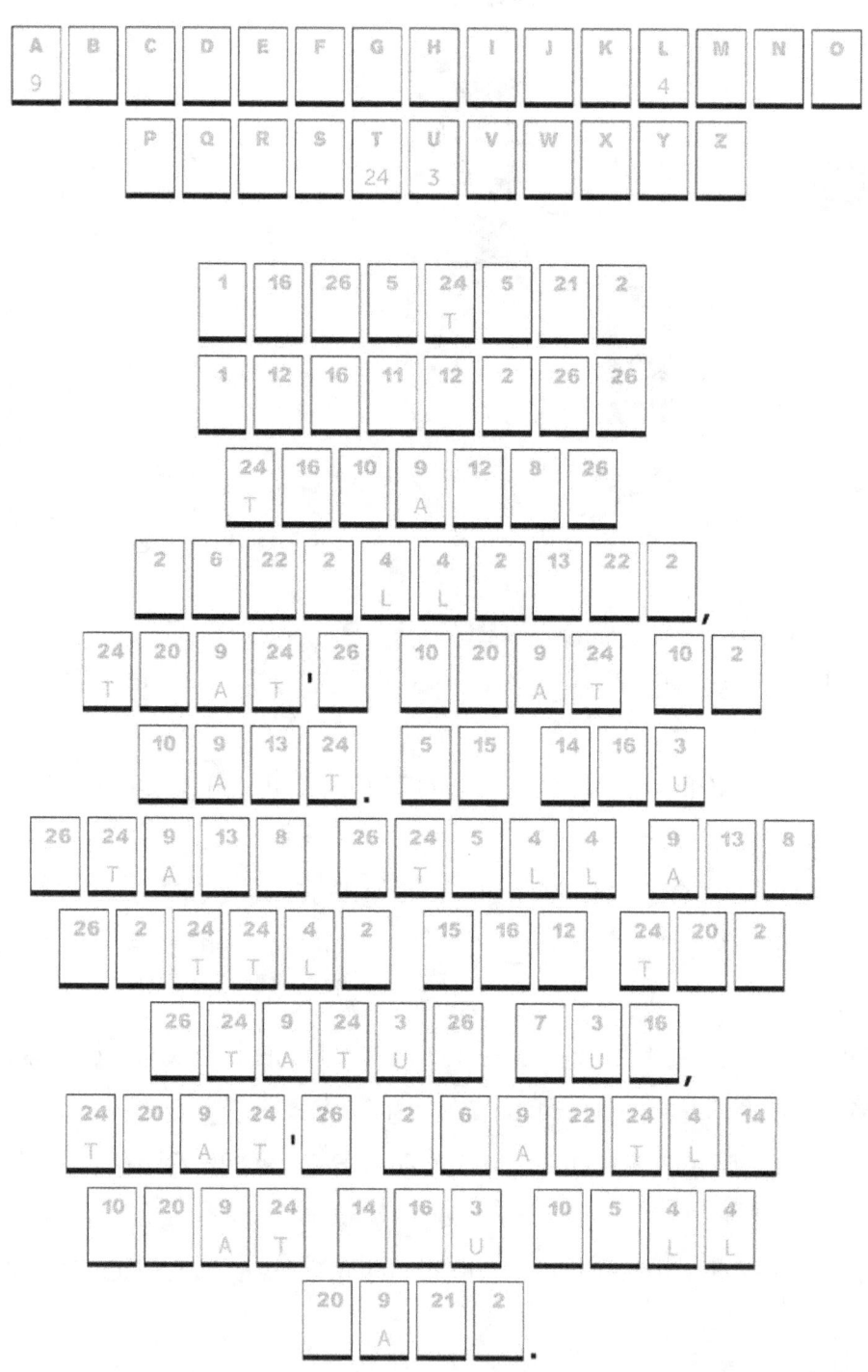

Daniel James Jr.

Daniel James Jr.

February 11, 1920 – February 25, 1978

OFFICER

LEFT BLANK ON PURPOSE

Daniel James Jr.

Daniel James Jr.

Daniel James Jr.

Daniel James Jr.

Daniel James Jr.

Daniel James Jr.

Hi, my name is Daniel James Jr. I was born on February 11, 1920, in Pensacola, FL. I graduated from Lillie A James School. I received a Bachelor of Science in Physical Education from Tuskegee University. As a youth, I inherited a lifelong nickname, "Chappie," from my older brother Charles. In 1943, I received my commission from the United States Army Air Force as a second lieutenant and my pilot's wings from Tuskegee Army Airfield. In 1950, during the Korean War, I flew 101 combat missions in F-51 Mustang and F-80 aircraft. In 1967, I flew 78 combat missions into North Vietnam, many of which were in the Hanoi/Haiphong region and led a flight in the "Operation Bolo" MiG sweep, in which seven Communist MiG-21s were destroyed. This mission had the highest total kill of any mission during the Vietnam War. In 1975, I was promoted to the rank of four-star general and became the highest-ranking African American in the history of the United States military to that date. I was promoted to commander in chief of NORAD/ADCOM.

1. What college did I go to?
   A. Howard University
   B. Tuskegee University
   C. Fisk University
2. What aircraft didn't I fly in the Korean War?
   A. F-51 Mustang
   B. P-47 Thunderbolt
   C. F-80
3. What year was I the highest ranking African-American?
   A. 1975
   B. 1967
   C. 1970

Directions: Answer the questions, to solve the crossword puzzle. You can use the internet if you get stuck on any question.

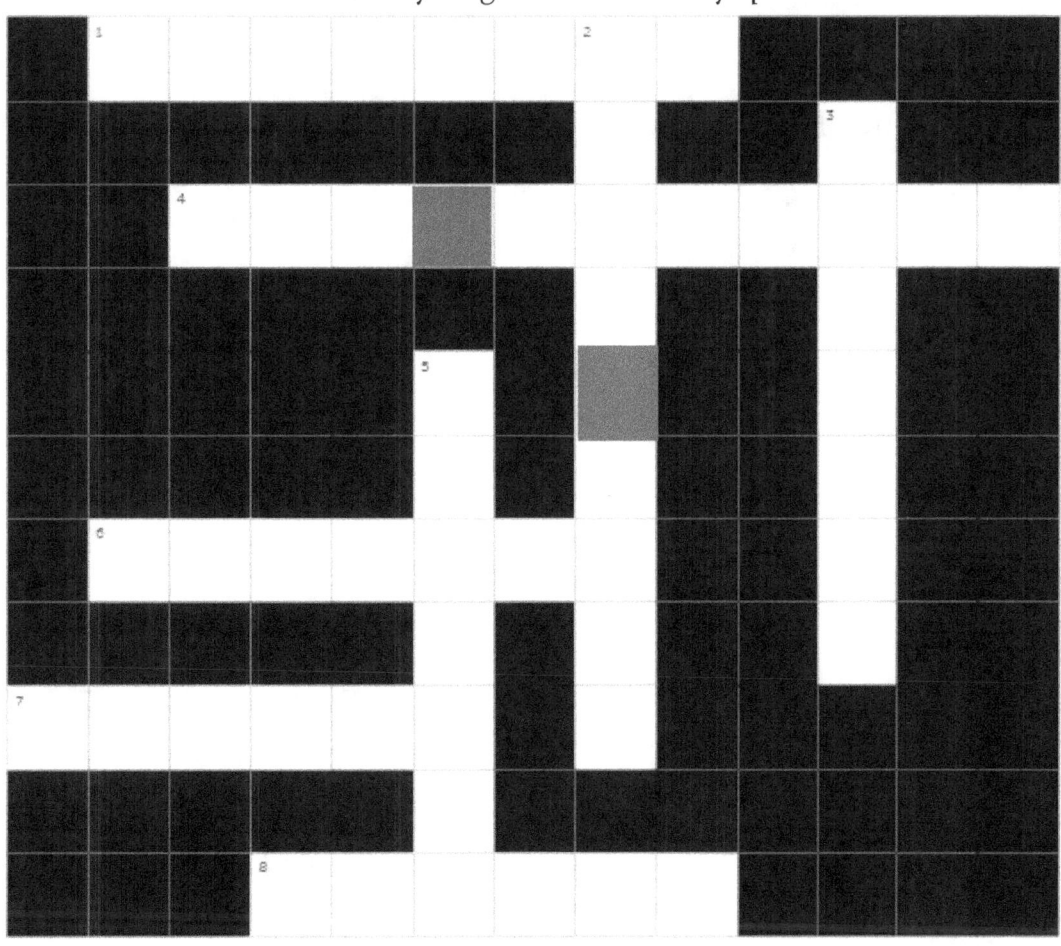

Across

1) Daniel flew the F-51 and F-80 _____ during his combat missions.

4) Daniel flew more than _____ combat missions.

6) Daniel had the _____ total kill of any mission during the Vietnam War with seven.

7) Daniel received the Distinguished Service Medal for his service in the ____ War.

8) Daniel completed fighter pilot ____ training at Selfridge Field, MI.

Down

2) Daniel was the first African American to reach the rank of ____ general in the United States Armed Forces.

3) Daniel was awarded the George Washington ____ Foundation Medal twice.

5) Daniel flew combat missions during the Korean War and ____ War. **167**

When was the United States Marine Corps established?

What branch of the military focuses on legal services and military justice?

What branch of the military is responsible for maintaining and operating military satellites?

Directions: Unscramble the words below about Daniel. See if you can get the bonus word.

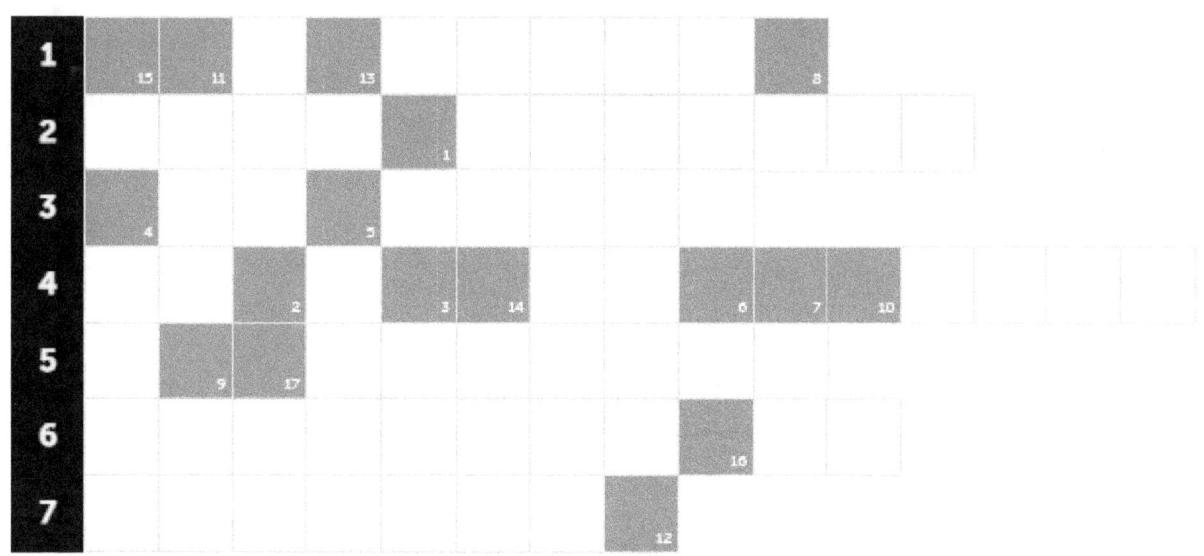

BONUS WORD

1	2	3	4	5	6	7	8

9	10	11	12	13	14	15	16	17

Unscramble Words

1) resuacriof   **2)** ritlhpitoefg   **3)** eoarakwnr

4) lurrnsgafoaerte   **5)** naraiewvmt   **6)** owrralowwdt

7) itl2pb5o

Directions: This is the WGLT Challenge. Solve the cryptogram. As the puzzle solver, you need to find which number belongs to which character. And this can be pretty challenging! You will need to match the number with the letter. There are some letters given to you below. This will help you solve the other words and unlock more characters. **Good Luck.**

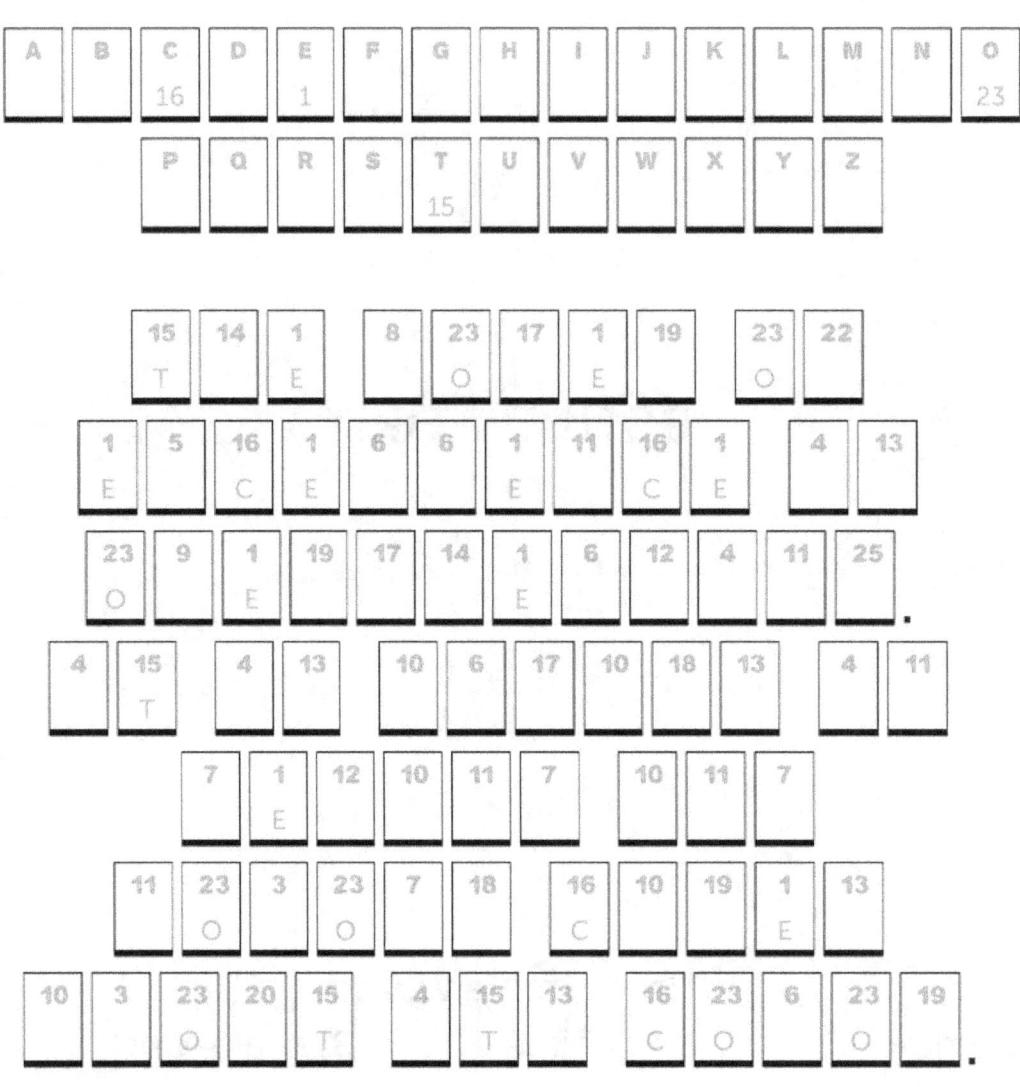

Roscoe Brown Jr.

Roscoe Brown Jr.

March 9, 1922 – July 2, 2016
TUSKEGEE AIRMEN

LEFT BLANK ON PURPOSE

Roscoe Brown Jr.

Roscoe Brown Jr.

Roscoe Brown Jr.

Roscoe Brown Jr.

Roscoe Brown Jr.

Roscoe Brown Jr.

Directions: read the bio below and answer the following questions.

Hi, my name is Roscoe Brown Jr. I was born on March 9, 1922, in Washington, D.C. I graduated from Dunbar High School. I earned my bachelor's degree from Springfield College. I joined the U.S. Army Air Force and graduated from the Tuskegee Flight School in 1944. I flew 68 combat missions, which comprised a combination of strafing runs and escort missions for heavy bombers and P-38 reconnaissance flights. In 1945, I was promoted to the rank of squadron commander. The success that the Tuskegee Airmen and I achieved in battle became a symbol of bravery and skill, which disproved the idea that Black people couldn't perform in the military, especially in roles that required advanced training. We became well-known for our stellar flying records and distinctive aircraft; we began breaking racial barriers abroad and eventually at home. In 1948, President Truman issued Executive Order 9981, which stated that "there shall be equality of treatment and opportunity for all persons in the armed forces without regard to race, color, religion, or national origin."

1. What degree did I get from Springfield College?
   A. Masters
   B. Bachelors
   C. Ph.D
2. In 1948, President Truman issued what?
   A. Cease fire
   B. Executive Order 9981
   C. Mandatory Draft
3. I was one of the original?
   A. Temptations
   B. Tuskegee Airmen
   C. Super Soldiers

Directions: Find the words associated with Roscoe's life and career.

3	3	2	N	D	F	I	G	H	T	E	R	G	R	O	U	P	P
D	Y	F	A	J	D	B	K	D	S	N	A	M	R	E	G	D	U
B	T	G	G	S	J	V	U	J	H	G	N	V	M	K	S	S	X
W	X	P	X	R	Z	J	P	K	J	S	Z	S	N	E	A	K	B
O	A	N	R	D	H	O	N	L	S	G	L	E	E	R	N	L	X
R	I	1	I	M	V	Q	Y	M	Y	D	T	N	M	N	X	C	U
L	A	L	5	A	I	W	F	H	H	E	G	Y	R	D	Q	O	Q
D	Q	H	I	-	T	O	J	I	E	S	W	O	I	F	X	M	G
W	W	I	P	M	P	P	I	Q	D	U	C	X	A	D	S	M	Y
A	O	A	R	P	H	L	A	X	T	X	K	R	E	N	Q	A	H
R	O	I	O	K	W	M	I	C	W	C	R	Z	E	C	Y	N	G
T	O	B	F	U	L	A	K	A	F	B	N	S	G	Z	H	D	K
W	H	M	E	U	M	B	F	X	T	Y	R	E	E	I	J	E	L
O	D	R	S	B	J	I	W	X	P	D	X	A	K	X	F	R	X
X	K	J	S	Q	E	V	Q	P	W	M	E	D	S	H	Y	O	P
S	C	A	O	Q	Y	N	J	Z	N	E	Z	R	U	S	J	E	L
O	J	M	R	W	G	U	A	N	I	M	M	M	T	R	M	A	F
Z	I	B	U	L	C	S	L	R	I	G	D	N	A	S	Y	O	B

Find These Words

USARMY   TUSKEGEEAIRMEN   REDTAILP-51

CAPTAIN   WORLDWARTWO   GERMAN

COMMANDER   332NDFIGHTERGROUP   BOYSANDGIRLSCLUB

PROFESSOR

What branch of the military is responsible for conducting search and rescue operations?

Which branch of the military focuses on psychological operations and information warfare?

What is the primary role of the United States Navy?

Directions: Read and answer the questions below. There are clues in the puzzle to help you. Try and solve the cryptic message.

Clue for cryptic message: Roscoe flew there.

Questions

1) Roscoe was a _____ at New York University.

2) Roscoe served as a _____ commander for the Tuskegee Airmen.

3) Roscoe received the Distinguished Flying ____ for his time in World War II.

4) Roscoe is the first 15th Air Force ____ to shoot down a jet.

5) Roscoe was a _____ in the U.S. Army Air Corps.

6) Roscoe flew 68 combat missions, a combination of strafing runs and _____ missions for heavy bombers and P-38 reconnaissance flights.

Directions: This is the WGLT Challenge. Solve the cryptogram. As the puzzle solver, you need to find which number belongs to which character. And this can be pretty challenging! You will need to match the number with the letter. There are some letters given to you below. This will help you solve the other words and unlock more characters. **Good Luck.**

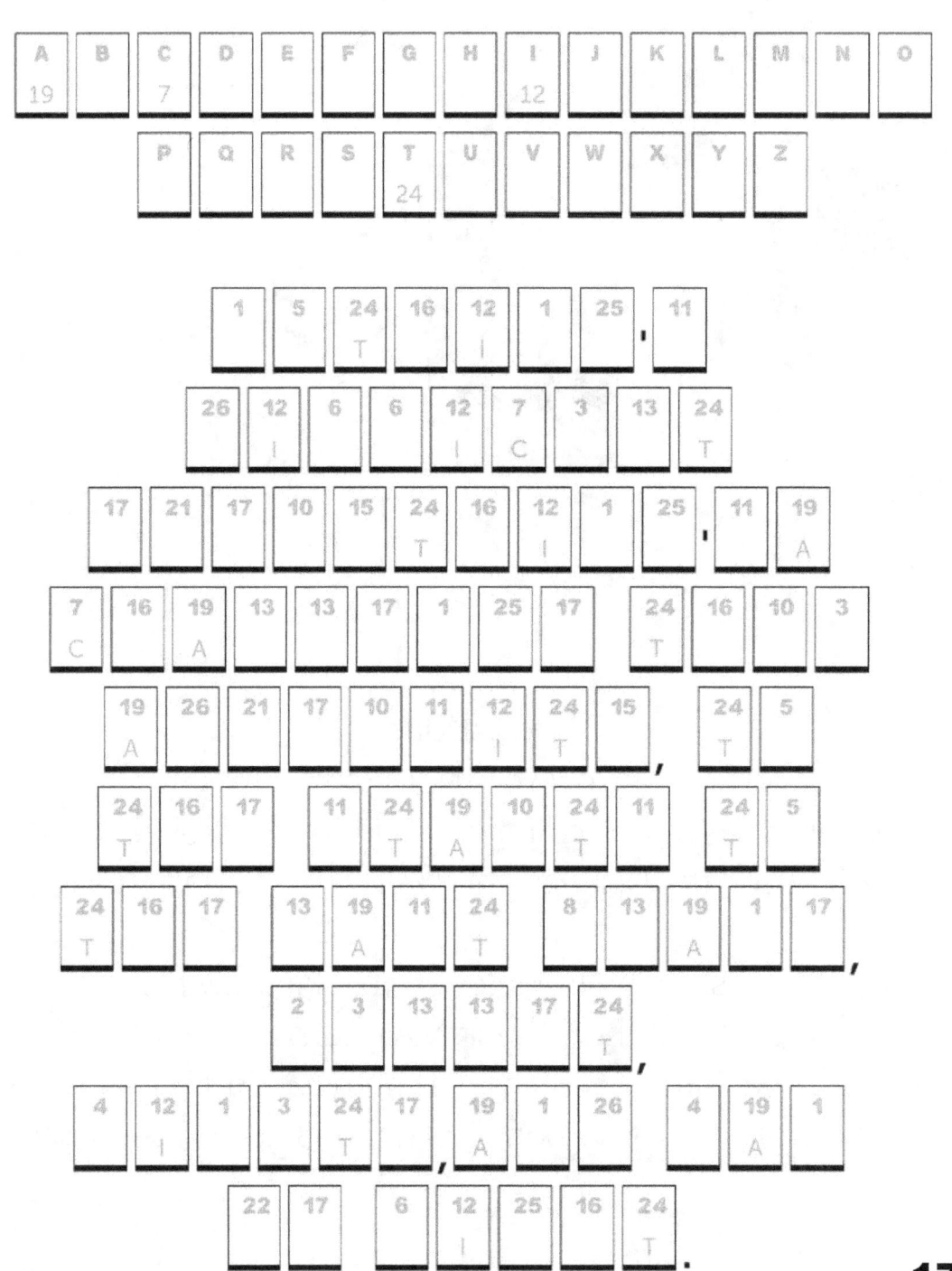

A	B	C	D	E	F	G	H	I	J	K	L	M	N	O
19		7						12						

P	Q	R	S	T	U	V	W	X	Y	Z
				24						

```
 1   5   24  16  12   1   25  , 11
         T       I

26  12   6   6   12   7   3   13  24
     I            I    C        T

17  21  17  10  15  24  16  12   1   25  , 11  19
                 T       I                     A

 7  16  19  13  13  17   1   25  17  24  16  10   3
 C       A                           T

19  26  21  17  10  11  12  24  15      24   5
 A                       I   T           T

24  16  17  11  24  19  10  24  11      24   5
 T               T   A       T           T

24  16  17  13  19  11  24   8  13  19   1  17  ,
 T               A   T                A

         2   3  13  13  17  24  ,
                         T

 4  12   1   3  24  17  19   1  26   4  19   1
     I           T       A            A

        22  17   6  12  25  16  24  .
                     I           T
```

178

Samuel Gravely Jr.

Samuel Gravely Jr.

June 4, 1922 – October 22, 2004

OFFICER **179**

LEFT BLANK ON PURPOSE

Samuel Gravely Jr.

Samuel Gravely Jr.

Samuel Gravely Jr.

Samuel Gravely Jr.

Samuel Gravely Jr.

Samuel Gravely Jr.

Directions: read the bio below and answer the following questions.

Hi, my name is Samuel Gravely Jr. I was born on June 4, 1922, in Richmond, VA. I was attending Virginia Union University when I enlisted in the U.S. Naval Reserve in 1942. In 1944, I completed Midshipmen's School at Columbia University and was commissioned as an ensign. During my first duty assignment, I was the only Black officer aboard the submarine chaser USS PC-1264, which had a predominantly Black crew. We were sent on this assignment for a test that was designed to measure the ability of African Americans to perform general Navy duties. In 1946, I was released from active duty but remained in the Naval Reserve. In 1948, I went back to Virginia Union University and earned my degree in history. I was recalled to active duty in 1949 during the Korean War. In 1961, I served as the first African American officer to command a U.S. Navy ship, the USS Theodore E. Chandler (DD-717). In 1966, I was the first African American to lead a ship into combat for the U.S. Navy. In 1967, I became the first African American to reach the rank of captain and in 1971, I was the first to reach the rank of rear admiral.

1. What was the name of the college I went to?
   A. Virginia Union University
   B. Hampton University
   C. Central State University
2. What year did I get recalled to the Navy?
   A. 1946
   B. 1949
   C. 1942
3. I was the first African American to lead?
   A. A Class room discusion
   B. A ship into combat
   C. A infantry unit into combat

Directions: Answer the questions, to solve the crossword puzzle. You can use the internet if you get stuck on any question.

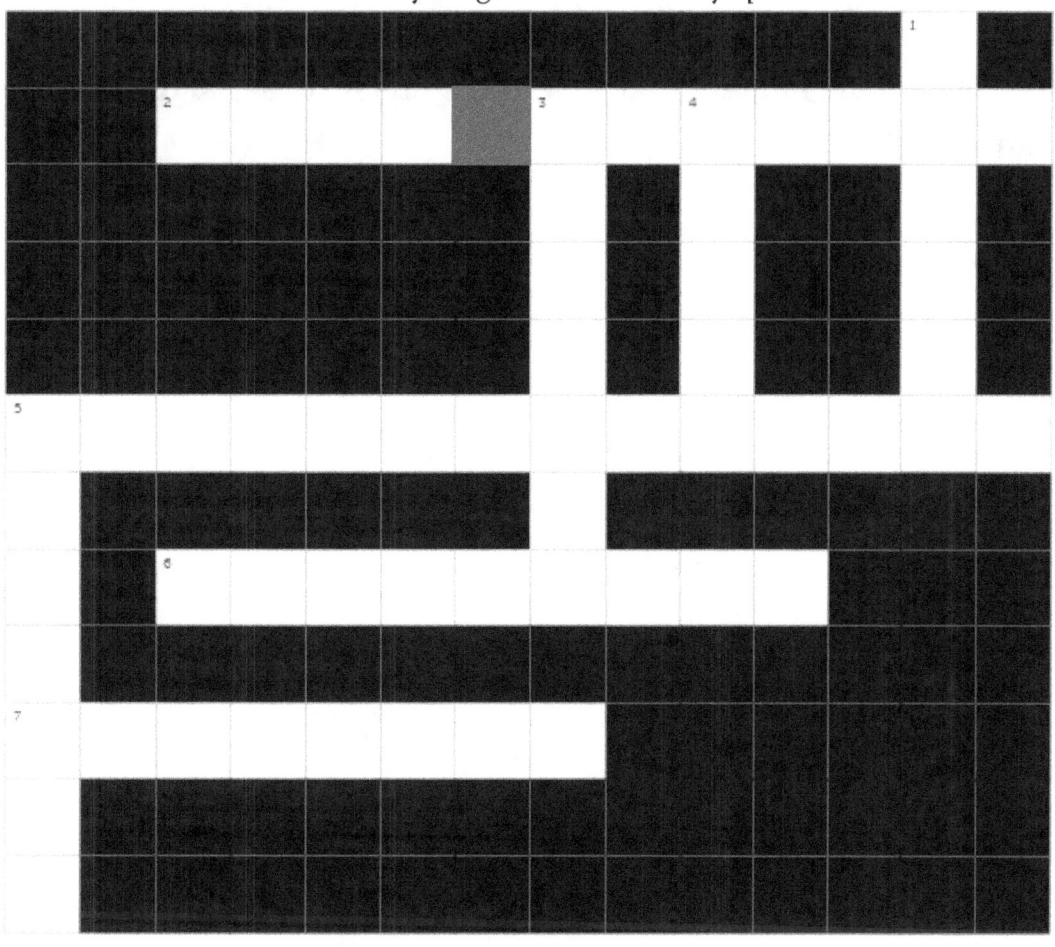

Across

2) Samuel was the first African American in the U.S. Navy to become a ___.

5) Samuel was the Director of Naval ___.

6) Samuel began his seagoing career as the only black officer aboard the ___ chaser USS PC-1264.

7) Samuel is honored ___ in San Pedro, California, aboard Battleship Iowa, at the Gravely Celebration Experience.

Down

1) Samuel was awarded the ___ of Merit.

3) Samuel was the first African American in the U.S. Navy to serve aboard a fighting ship as an ___.

4) Samuel was the first African American in the U.S. Navy to become a ___ commander.

5) Samuel was the first African American in the U.S. Navy to __ a Navy ship.

183

Directions: Read and answer the questions. These are your opinions so the answers will vary.

Which branch of the military is known for its precision aerial displays and demonstrations?

What is the primary role of the United States Coast Guard?

What do you think you might be doing in 10 years?

Directions: Unscramble the words below about Samuel. See if you can get the bonus word.

	9				13					
1										
2		11		8		5				3
3							17			
4						7				14
5		10		12	18					
6	4						2			
7			13							
8	6			16	1					

BONUS WORD

1	2	3	4	5	6	7	8

9	10	11	12	13	14	15	16	17	18

Unscramble Words

1) snsasoum

2) aeriavmidcl

3) orwdwrwalto

4) fceiflgfora

5) naysuv

6) fouuitsgsa

7) krwaranoe

8) eceinrb

Directions: This is the WGLT Challenge. Solve the cryptogram. As the puzzle solver, you need to find which number belongs to which character. And this can be pretty challenging! You will need to match the number with the letter. There are some letters given to you below. This will help you solve the other words and unlock more characters. **Good Luck.**

A	B	C	D	E	F	G	H	I	J	K	L	M	N	O
16					25								4	12

P	Q	R	S	T	U	V	W	X	Y	Z

| 1 | 21 | 26 | 4(N) | | 10 | 12(O) | 19 | | 22 | 11 | 16(A) | 4(N) | 23 |

| 16(A) | 4(N) | 23 | | 25(F) | 9 | 5 | 21 | 11 | | 25(F) | 12(O) | 20 |

| 16(A) | 3 | 26 | 20 | 9 | 14 | 16(A) | | 10 | 12(O) | 19 | , | 20 | 26 |

| 23 | 26 | 25(F) | 26 | 4(N) | 23 | 9 | 4(N) | 5 | | 16(A) | 4(N) |

| 16(A) | 3 | 26 | 20 | 9 | 14 | 16(A) | | 11 | 21 | 16(A) | 11 | | 9 | 22 |

| 4(N) | 12(O) | 11 | | 2 | 26 | 20 | 25(F) | 26 | 14 | 11 | | 18 | 19 | 11 | ... |

| 9 | 11 | , | 22 | | 18 | 26 | 11 | 11 | 26 | 20 | | 11 | 21 | 16(A) | 4(N) |

| 16(A) | 4(N) | 10 | | 12(O) | 11 | 21 | 26 | 20 |

| 14 | 12(O) | 19 | 4(N) | 11 | 20 | 10 | | 9 | | 15 | 4(N) | 12(O) | 1 | . |

Guion Bluford Jr.

Guion Bluford Jr.

November 22, 1942 - PRESENT

AEROSPACE ENGINEER

187

LEFT BLANK ON PURPOSE

Guion Bluford Jr.

Guion Bluford Jr.

Guion Bluford Jr.

Guion Bluford Jr.

Guion Bluford Jr.

Guion Bluford Jr.

Directions: read the bio below and answer the following questions.

Hi, my name is Guion Bluford Jr. I was born on November 22, 1942, in Philadelphia, PA. I graduated from Overbrook High School. I received a Bachelor of Science in Aerospace Engineering from Pennsylvania State University. I got my Master of Science in Aerospace Engineering from the U.S. Air Force Institute of Technology (AFIT). I received my Ph.D. in Aerospace Engineering from AFIT. I also got my Master of Business Administration degree from the University of Houston-Clear Lake. After I got my commission, I received my pilot's wings in 1966. I flew more than 140 combat missions in the Vietnam War while logging more than 5,200 hours in various aircraft, including the F-15 Eagle, F-4C Phantom II, U-2 and F-5A. In 1978, I was selected to become a NASA astronaut. In 1979, I was officially designated as an astronaut. In 1983, I became the first African American to become an astronaut and go to space in an STS-8.

1. What is the highest degree I have gotten?
   A. Masters Degree
   B. Ph.D
   C. Bachelors Degree
2. What year did I get my pilot wings?
   A. 1960
   B. 1966
   C. 1963
3. I was the first African American to do what?
   A. Become an pilot
   B. Become an soldier
   C. Become an astronaut

Directions: Find the words associated with Guion's life and career.

```
Z  G  O  Y  K  X  G  V  P  D  A  P  J  D  Y  Q  U  W
A  E  R  O  S  P  A  C  E  E  N  G  I  N  E  E  R  I
Q  X  B  X  I  S  I  U  W  R  K  Z  E  P  T  H  T  V
K  B  I  Q  K  N  E  Y  S  D  Y  A  A  V  N  D  U  T
C  L  T  R  C  K  Z  F  Z  P  G  W  I  X  A  Q  A  T
U  G  E  L  D  H  H  Z  K  L  A  E  C  I  H  V  N  T
W  R  R  H  Q  C  P  R  E  L  T  C  I  W  E  V  O  O
E  Y  C  K  I  U  X  S  K  N  R  R  E  O  O  Q  R  L
P  F  H  G  M  D  C  V  A  I  C  C  I  B  O  F  T  I
E  U  A  M  K  O  Z  M  O  L  P  A  E  C  P  F  S  P
N  G  L  J  U  H  W  O  L  T  I  G  N  E  Y  Q  A  R
N  A  L  T  U  A  E  C  R  O  F  R  I  A  S  U  A  E
S  V  E  H  R  V  L  B  Y  U  Q  X  I  F  X  F  S  T
T  L  N  Z  U  A  Z  S  Q  K  G  K  P  X  F  D  A  H
A  I  G  T  A  S  L  B  B  L  C  O  H  R  P  F  N  G
T  V  E  H  A  H  I  Z  T  U  Z  F  V  K  S  N  F  I
E  U  R  F  C  O  L  O  N  E  L  J  M  Q  S  U  L  F
C  F  S  N  B  E  S  K  D  N  C  Y  K  J  R  K  X  V
```

Find These Words

USAIRFORCE   SPACE   COLONEL

ORBITERCHALLENGER   NASAASTRONAUT   AEROSPACEENGINEER

FIGHTERPILOT   VIETNAMWAR   PENNSTATE

EAGLESCOUT

What is the primary role of the United States military?

Which branch of the military is known for its elite special operations forces, such as the Navy SEALs and Green Berets?

Which branch of the military focuses on providing medical services to personnel?

Directions: Read and answer the questions below. There are clues in the puzzle to help you. Try and solve the cryptic message.

Clue for cryptic message: Guion has been here before.

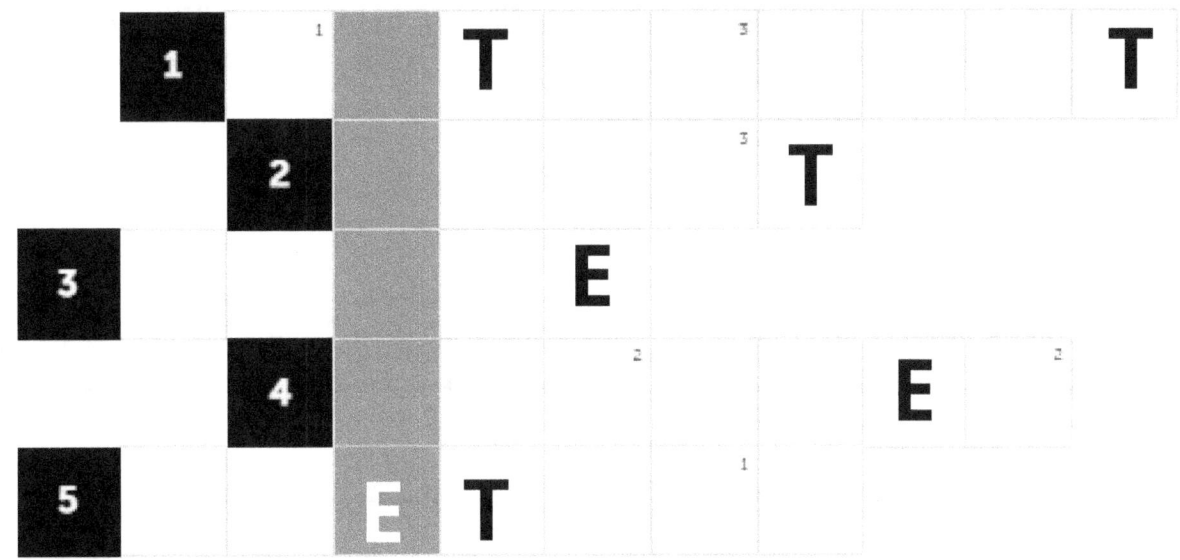

Questions

1) Guion was selected to become a NASA ____ in 1978 as a part of NASA astronaut group 8.

2) Guion was an U.S. Air Force officer and fighter ___.

3) Guion the first African American in ___.

4) Guion was a ___ in the U.S. Air Force.

5) Guion flew 144 combat missions during the ___ War.

Directions: This is the WGLT Challenge. Solve the cryptogram. As the puzzle solver, you need to find which number belongs to which character. And this can be pretty challenging! You will need to match the number with the letter. There are some letters given to you below. This will help you solve the other words and unlock more characters. **Good Luck.**

Milton Olive III

Milton Olive III

November 7, 1946 – October 22, 1965
SOLDIER

LEFT BLANK ON PURPOSE

Milton Olive III

Milton Olive III

Milton Olive III

Milton Olive III

Milton Olive III

Milton Olive III

Hi, my name is Milton Olive III. I was born on November 7, 1946, in Chicago, IL. I was 18 when I enlisted in the Army and became a U.S. Army paratrooper. In 1963, the U.S. Army's 173rd Airborne Brigade became the first major combat unit to arrive in Vietnam. As the Army's only action-ready unit in the Pacific at that time, we patrolled near Phu Cuong in 1965. As we moved through jungle brush, we tried to spot Viet Cong operating in the area. We were quietly and steadily pursuing one band of Viet Cong through the tangled growth. Suddenly, one of the enemies turned and threw a hand grenade into the middle of the platoon. I dashed forward and grabbed the grenade. Yelling, "I've got it," I tucked it into my shirt and moved away from the others, fell onto the grenade and absorbed the full blast. I sacrificed myself to save my fellow soldiers' lives. In 1966, President Lyndon B. Johnson presented my Medal of Honor to my father and stepmother. Posthumously, I became the first African American recipient of the Medal of Honor.

1. What did I become when I joined the Army?
   A. Tank Driver
   B. Mess Hall staff
   C. Paratrooper
2. What war did I fight in?
   A. Korean War
   B. World War II
   C. Vietnam War
3. I was the first African-American to do what?
   A. Get the Medal of Honor
   B. Get the Navy Cross
   C. Get the Purple Heart

Directions: Answer the questions, to solve the crossword puzzle. You can use the internet if you get stuck on any question.

Across

2) Milton sacrificed his life to save others by falling on a _____, while patrolling in Viet Cong.

4) Milton was a member of the _____ of Company B during the Vietnam War.

5) Milton was a PFC in the U.S. _____.

6) Milton was the first African-American recipient of the ___.

Down

1) Milton has a statue in the African-American Medal of Honor Recipients _____ in Wilmington, Delaware.

3) President _____ presented Milton's Medal of Honor to his father and stepmother.

Which branch of the military specializes in explosive ordnance disposal?

What is the primary mission of the United States Cyber Command?

What is the primary role of the United States Army Reserve?

Directions: Unscramble the words below about Milton Lee. See if you can get the bonus word.

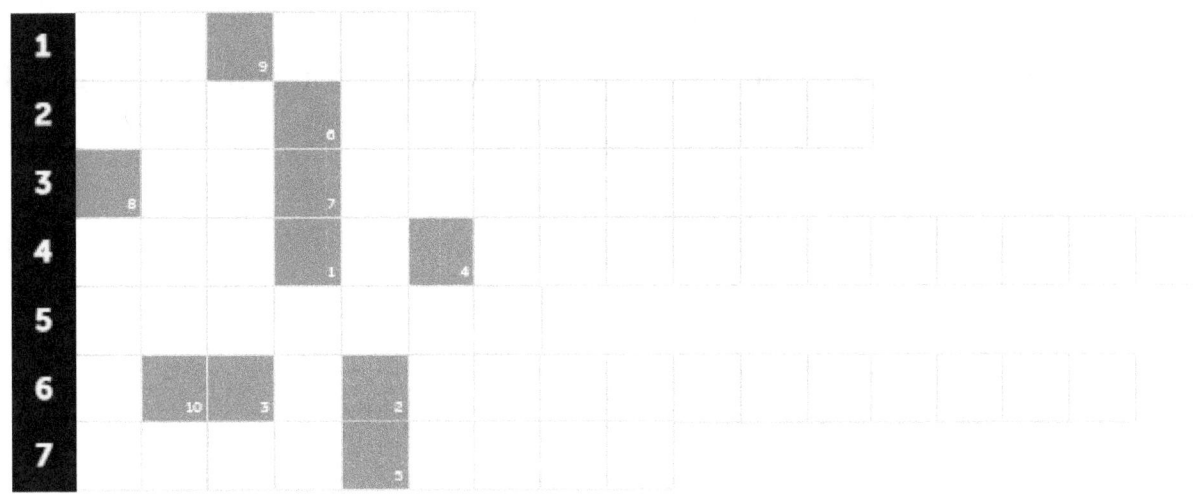

BONUS WORD

1	2	3	4	5	6	7		8	9	10

Unscramble Words

1) suayrm

2) elmahforodno

3) ownnitmgli

4) acsirlptefarvists

5) cgaohci

6) sooneipnnrjhetds

7) nlgoxneti

Directions: This is the WGLT Challenge. Solve the cryptogram. As the puzzle solver, you need to find which number belongs to which character. And this can be pretty challenging! You will need to match the number with the letter. There are some letters given to you below. This will help you solve the other words and unlock more characters. **Good Luck.**

1. **Which skill didn't I learn when I was young?**
   A. Rigger
   B. Sail Maker
   C. Singer
2. **What war did I become a Captain in?**
   A. Civil War
   B. World War I
   C. World War II
3. **What was the name of the ship I was a Captain of?**
   A. USS Onward
   B. CSS Planter
   C. USS Keokuk

Robert Smalls

Answers

1 BEAUFORT
2 CIVILWAR
3 REPUBLICAN
4 UNIONARMY
5 PRESIDENTLINCOLN
6 PUBLISHER
7 POLITICIAN
8 SLAVERY
9 CSSPLANTER

U S HOUSE

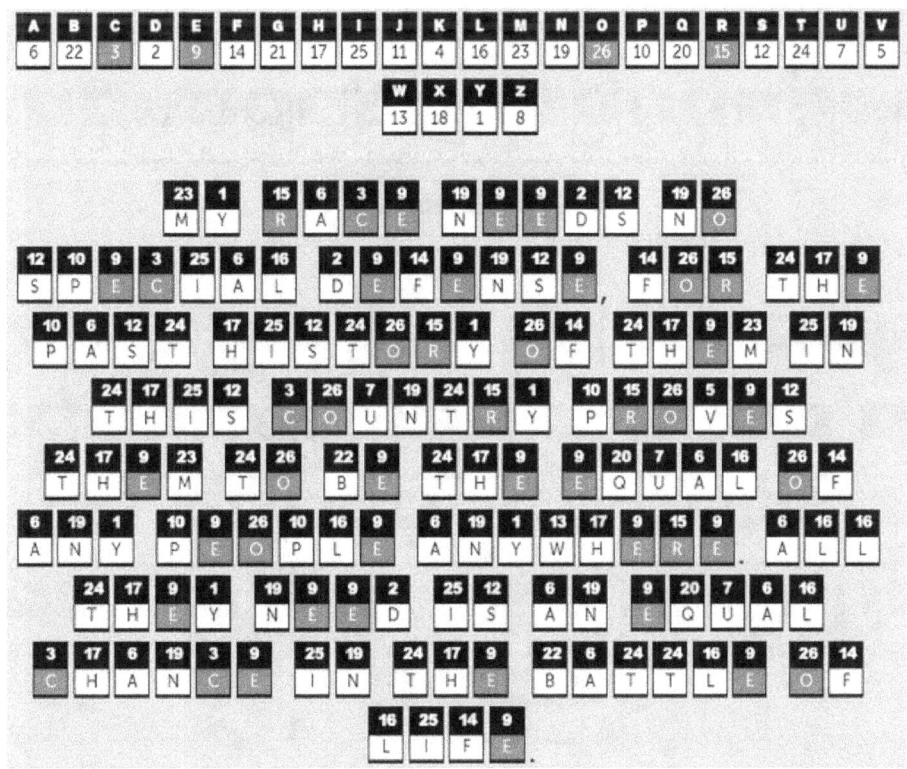

MY RACE NEEDS NO SPECIAL DEFENSE, FOR THE PAST HISTORY OF THEM IN THIS COUNTRY PROVES THEM TO BE THE EQUAL OF ANY PEOPLE ANYWHERE. ALL THEY NEED IS AN EQUAL CHANCE IN THE BATTLE OF LIFE.

203

1. I founded the first free African-American school for?
   A. Everybody
   B. Children
   C. Adults

2. I help in the recovery of _____ as a nurse in the Civil War?
   A. Smallpox
   B. Chickenpox
   C. Polio

3. I was the first African-American woman to do what?
   A. Teach a free nursing school in Georgia
   B. Teach a free school in Georgia
   C. Teach a free school in Alabama

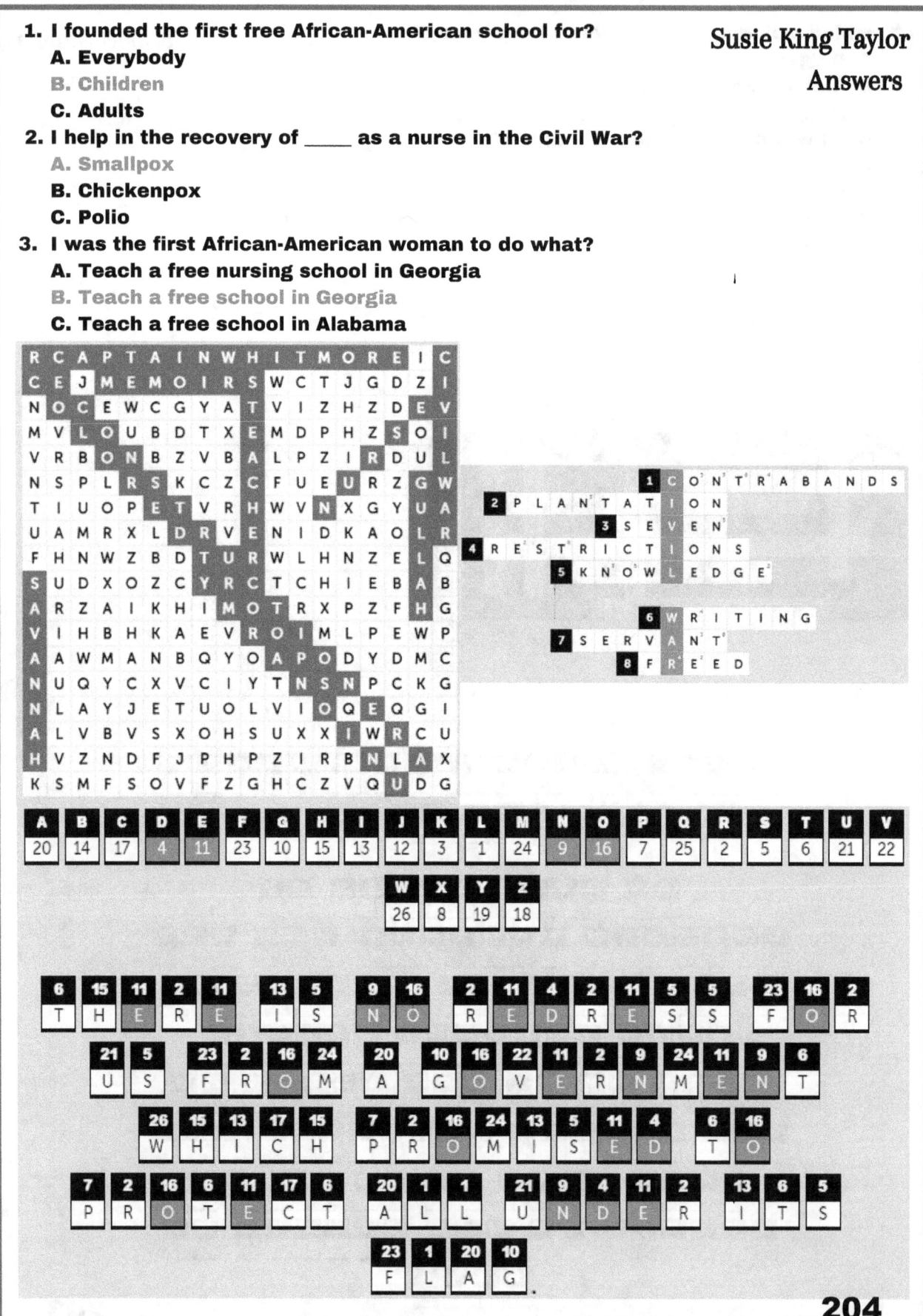

1 CONTRABANDS
2 PLANTATION
3 SEVEN
4 RESTRICTIONS
5 KNOWLEDGE
6 WRITING
7 SERVANT
8 FREED

A	B	C	D	E	F	G	H	I	J	K	L	M	N	O	P	Q	R	S	T	U	V
20	14	17	4	11	23	10	15	13	12	3	1	24	9	16	7	25	2	5	6	21	22

W	X	Y	Z
26	8	19	18

THERE IS NO REDRESS FOR

US FROM A GOVERNMENT

WHICH PROMISED TO

PROTECT ALL UNDER ITS

FLAG.

204

1. **What branch of the military did I join?**
   A. United States Navy
   B. United States Army
   C. United States Air Force
2. **Which aircraft didn't I pilot?**
   A. Bell P-39Q Airacobra
   B. Republic P-47D Thunderbolt
   C. Boeing B-17 Flying Fortress
3. **What fraternity ddi I belong to?**
   A. Alpha Phi Alpha
   B. Omega Psi Phi
   C. Phi Beta Sigma

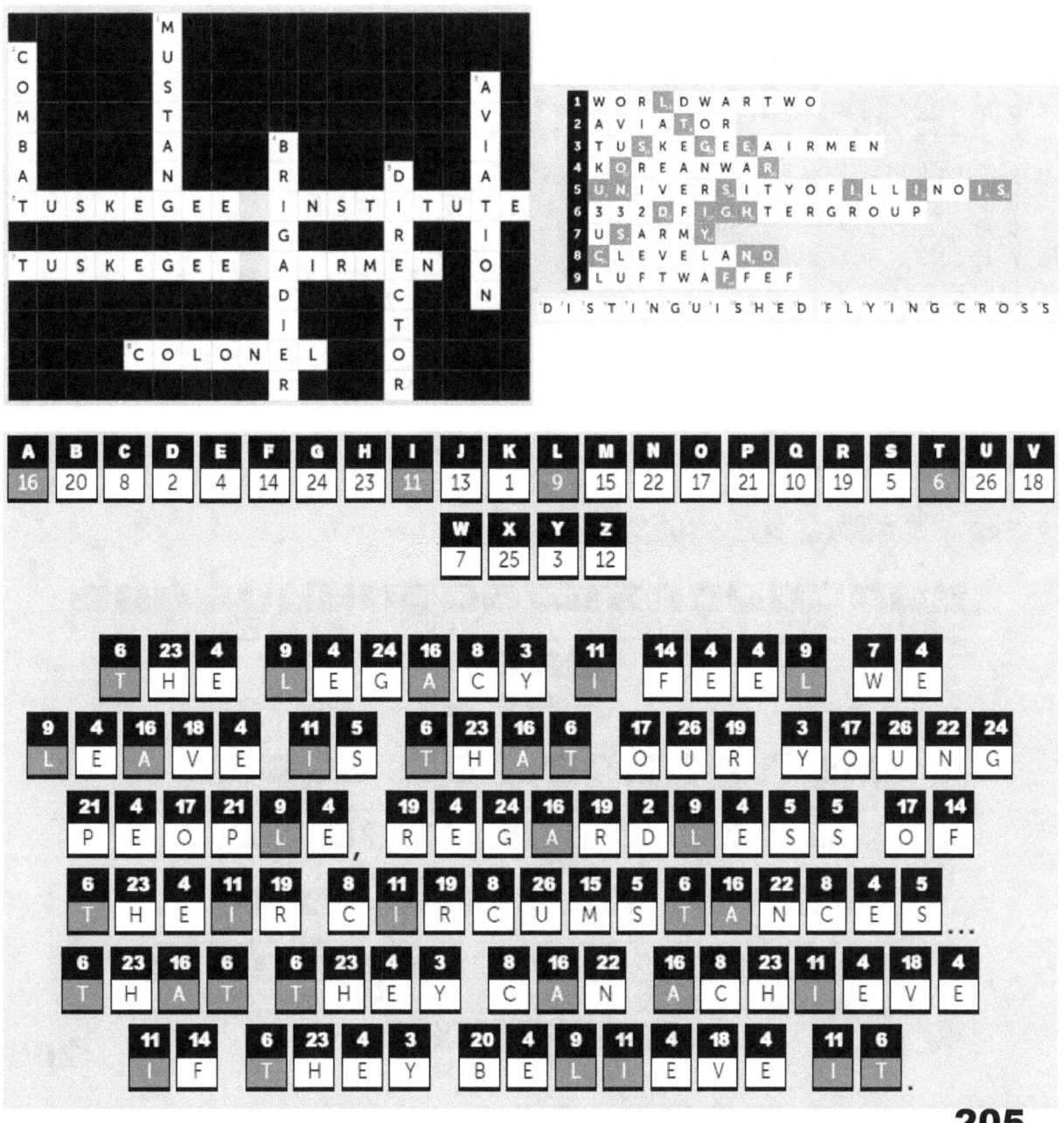

1. **What musical was I apart of when I was a young teen?**
   A. Exposition des Arts Décoratifs
   B. The Chocolate Dandies
   C. Shuffle Along
2. **What was my rank in the Free French Forces Air Force?**
   A. 2nd Lieutenant
   B. 1st Lieutenant
   C. Major
3. **Who was I a spy for?**
   A. United States
   B. French
   C. Germany

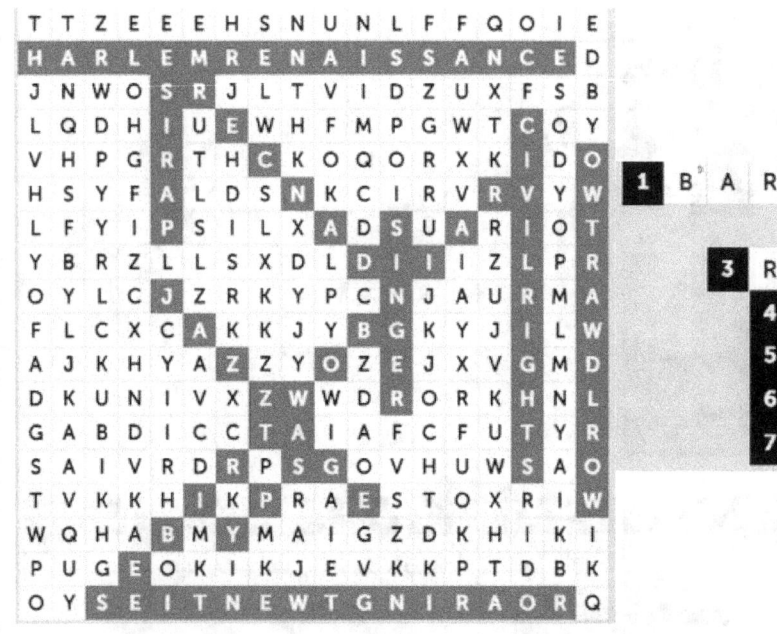

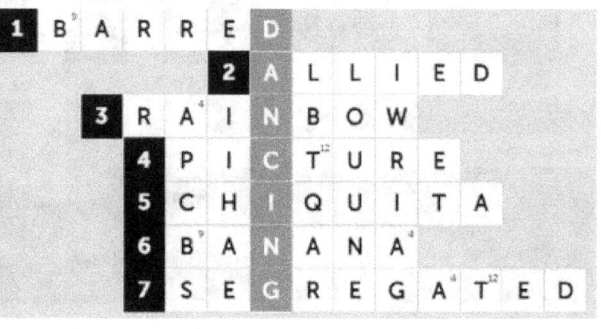

1. BARRED
2. ALLIED
3. RAINBOW
4. PICTURE
5. CHIQUITA
6. BANANA
7. SEGREGATED

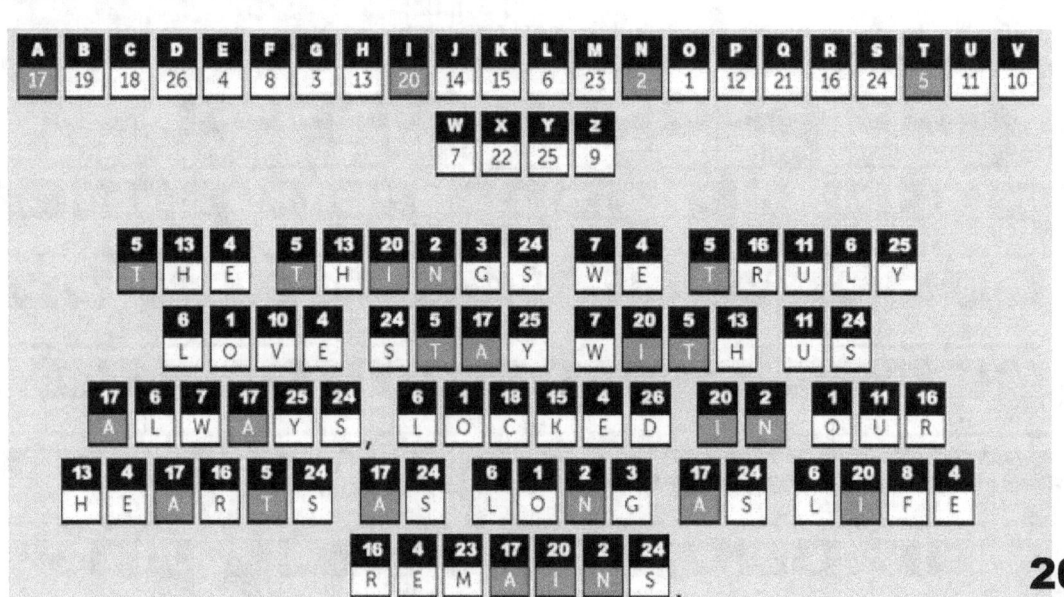

A	B	C	D	E	F	G	H	I	J	K	L	M	N	O	P	Q	R	S	T	U	V
17	19	18	26	4	8	3	13	20	14	15	6	23	2	1	12	21	16	24	5	11	10

W	X	Y	Z
7	22	25	9

THE THINGS WE TRULY

LOVE STAY WITH US

ALWAYS, LOCKED IN OUR

HEARTS AS LONG AS LIFE

REMAINS.

206

1. **What is the nickname of the 369th Infantry Regiment?**
   A. Black Death
   B. Harlem Hellfighters
   C. NY Killers
2. **What year did I fight off the Germans?**
   A. 1918
   B. 1917
   C. 1920
3. **I was the first U.S. soldier in World War I to receive?**
   A. Purple Heart
   B. Medal of Honor
   C. Croix de guerre

William Henry Johnson

Answers

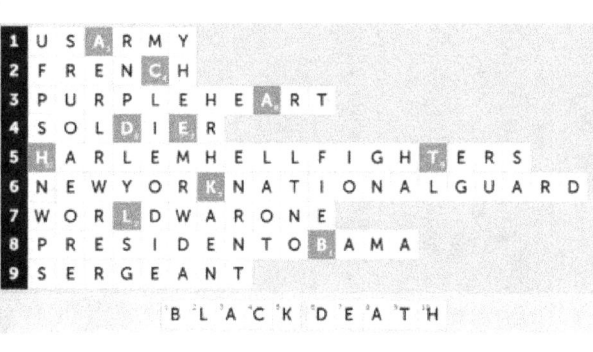

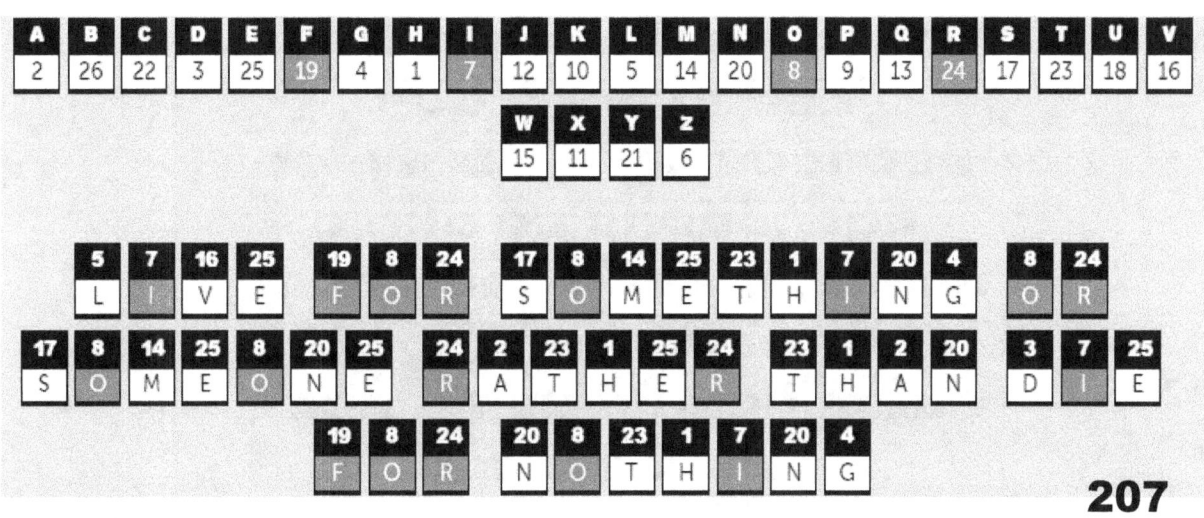

A	B	C	D	E	F	G	H	I	J	K	L	M	N	O	P	Q	R	S	T	U	V
2	26	22	3	25	19	4	1	7	12	10	5	14	20	8	9	13	24	17	23	18	16

W	X	Y	Z
15	11	21	6

L I V E   F O R   S O M E T H I N G   O R
S O M E O N E   R A T H E R   T H A N   D I E
F O R   N O T H I N G

207

1. **Which college did I graduate from?**
   A. Kansas State College
   B. University of Kansas
   C. Wichita State University

2. **What year did I urge black women to get in uniform?**
   A. 1945
   B. 1942
   C. 1943

3. **What was my highest rank in the WAC?**
   A. First Lieutenant
   B. Lieutenant Colonel
   C. Major

1. ADVISOR
2. COLONEL
3. AGRICULTURE
4. MAJOR
5. MEMORANDUMS
6. DEPRESSION
7. REPRESENT
8. SOLDIERS

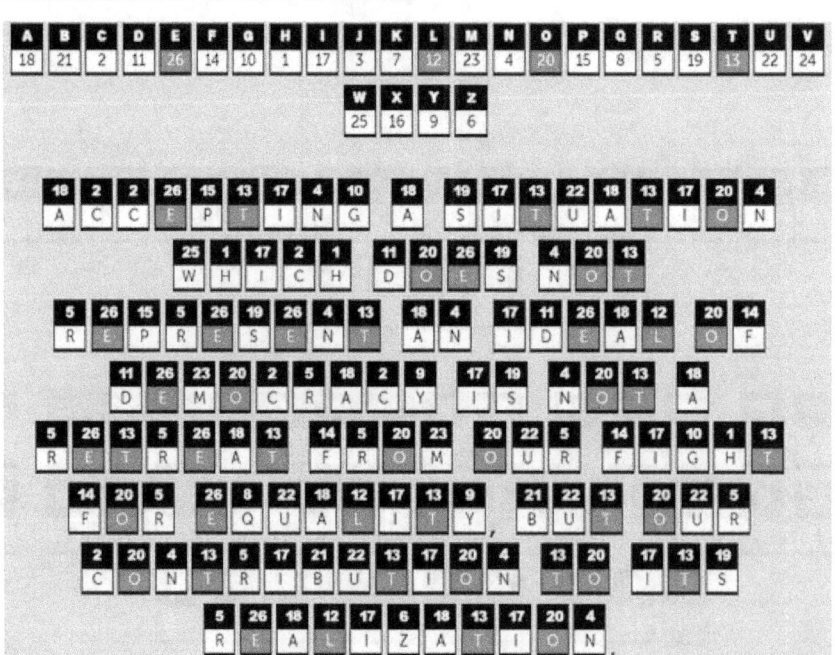

A	B	C	D	E	F	G	H	I	J	K	L	M	N	O	P	Q	R	S	T	U	V
18	21	2	11	26	14	10	1	17	3	7	12	23	4	20	15	8	5	19	13	22	24

W	X	Y	Z
25	16	9	6

ACCEPTING A SITUATION
WHICH DOES NOT
REPRESENT AN IDEAL OF
DEMOCRACY IS NOT A
RETREAT FROM OUR FIGHT
FOR EQUALITY, BUT OUR
CONTRIBUTION TO ITS
REALIZATION.

208

1. **Which college did I get my Masters from?**
   A. City College of New York
   B. Reserve Officers Training Corps
   C. George Washington University
2. **What year did I become Secretary of State?**
   A. 2005
   B. 2001
   C. 1989
3. **What my highest rank in the military?**
   A. Lieutenant General
   B. Brigadier General
   C. General

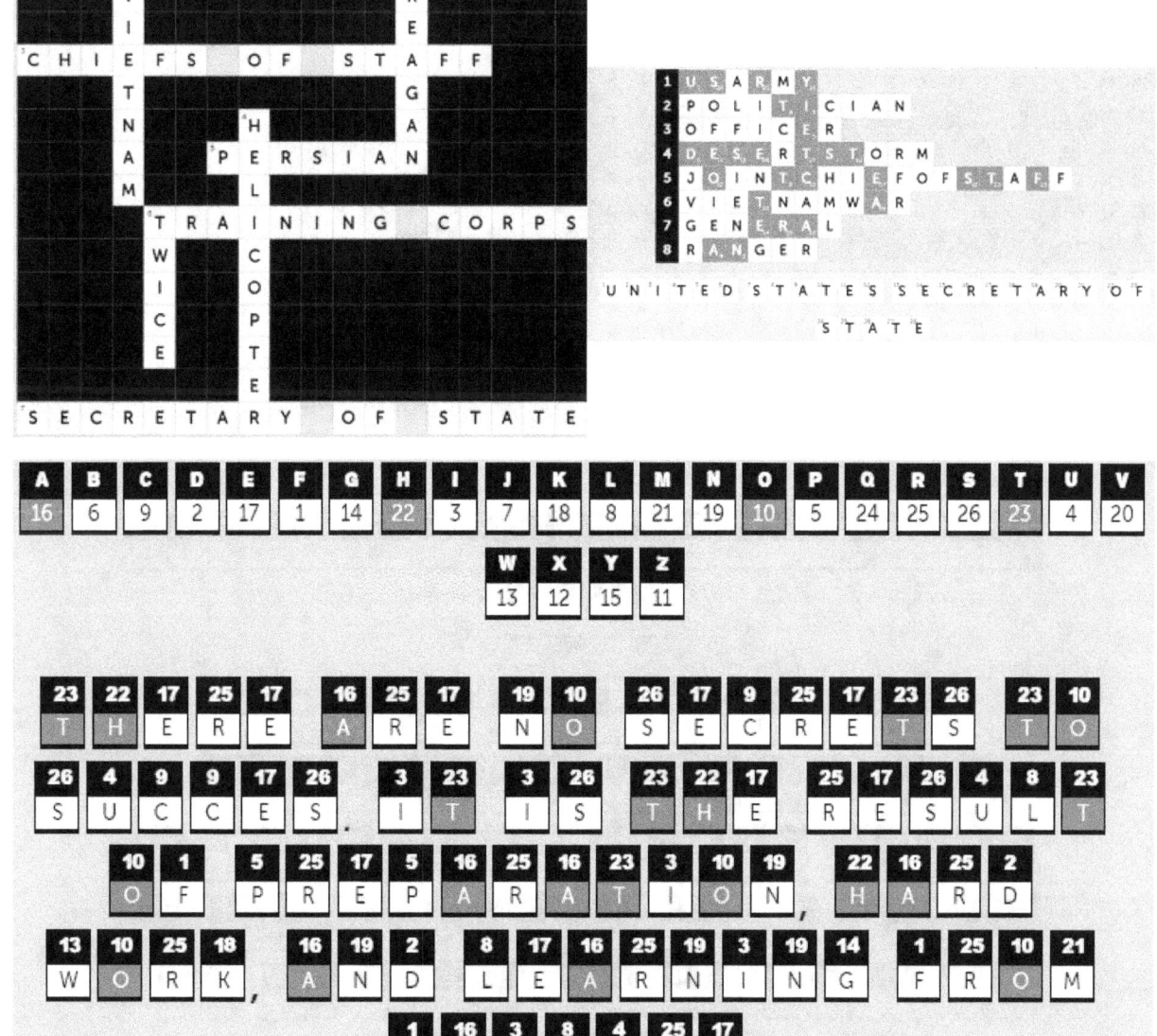

1. **What year did I get my commission?**
   A. 2018
   B. 1985
   C. 1991

2. **Which college didn't I go to?**
   A. University of Oklahoma
   B. University of New York
   C. Marquette University

3. **I was the first black woman to do what?**
   A. Promotion to brigadier general in the USMC
   B. Promotion to brigadier general in the USN
   C. Promotion to brigadier general in the USAF

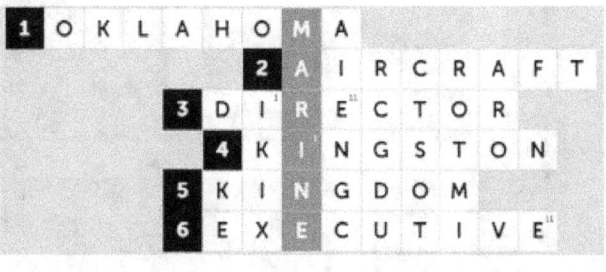

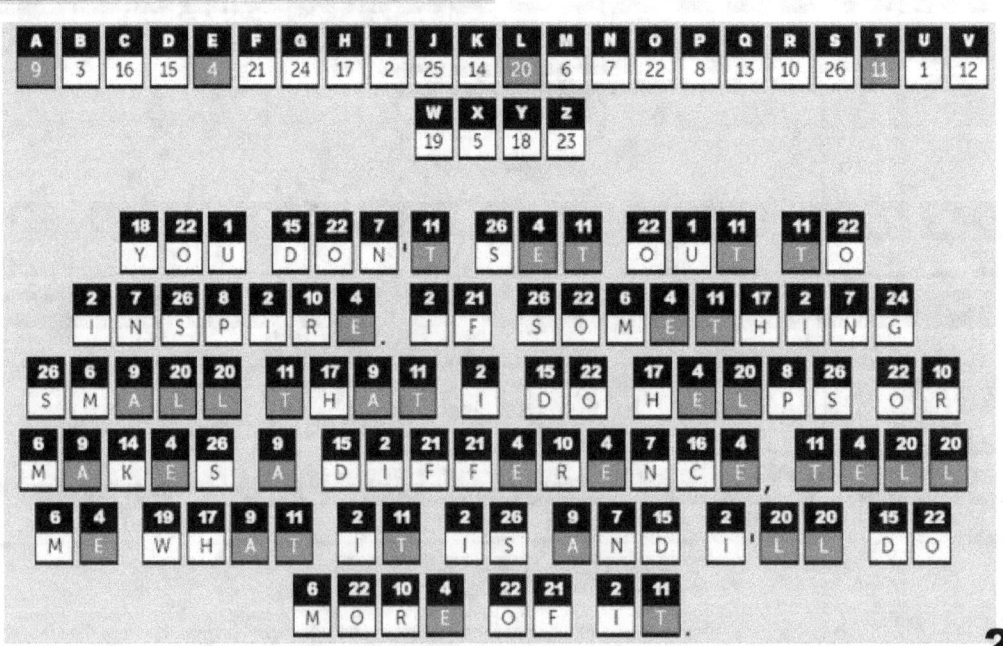

YOU DON'T SET OUT TO INSPIRE. IF SOMETHING SMALL THAT I DO HELPS OR MAKES A DIFFERENCE, TELL ME WHAT IT IS AND I'LL DO MORE OF IT.

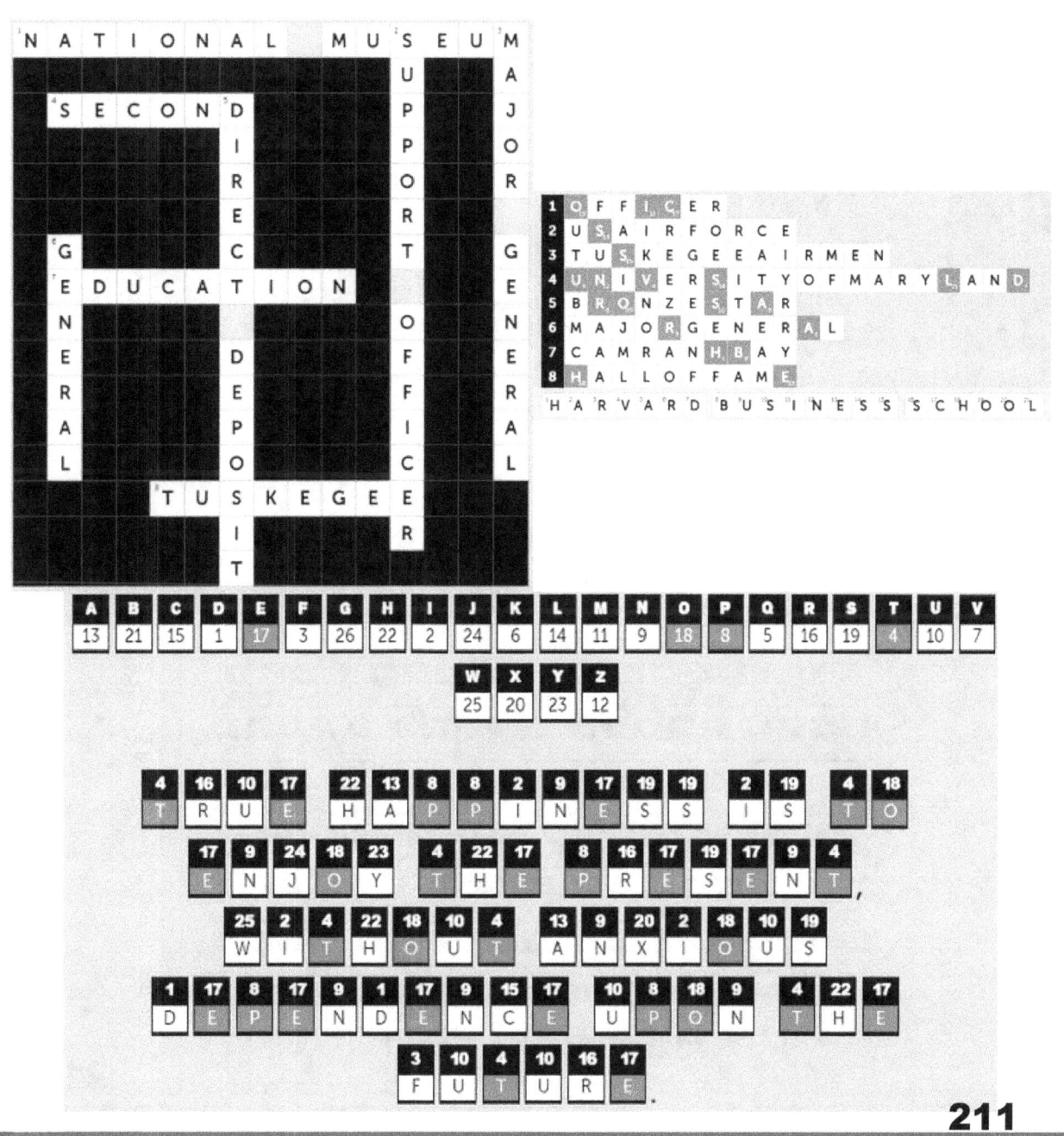

1. **What rank did I come in the Air Force as?**
   A. 2nd Lieutenant
   B. Private
   C. Private First Class
2. **What year did I graduate Officer Candidate School?**
   A. 1946
   B. 1942
   C. 1950
3. **Which war didn't I fight In?**
   A. Korean War
   B. Vietnam War
   C. World War I

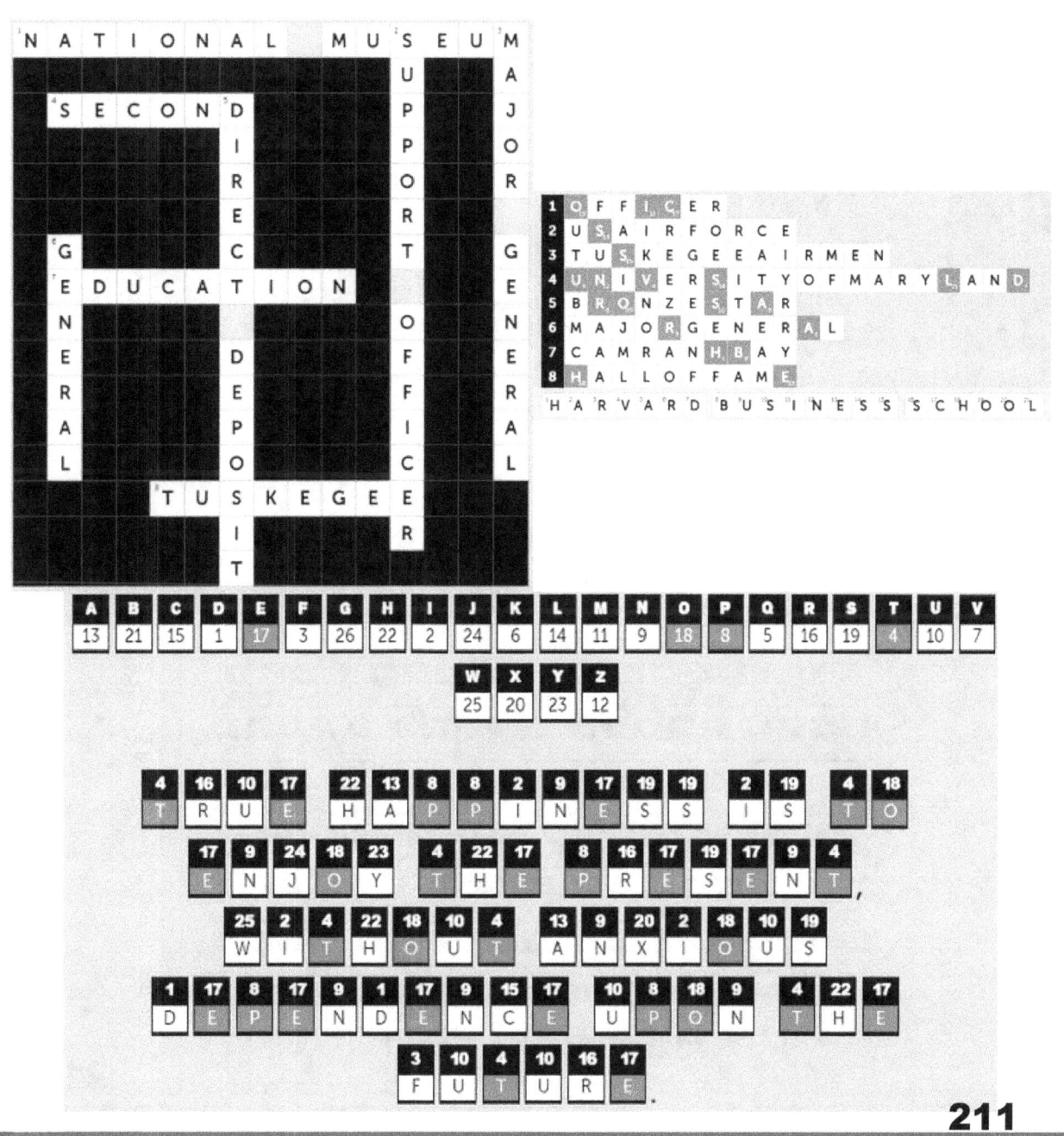

Lucius Theus

Answers

211

Marcelite J. Harris

Answers

1. **What college did I get my Bachelors degree from?**
   A. Voorhees College
   B. Spelman College
   C. Bennett College
2. **What is my highest rank in the Air Force?**
   A. Brigadier General
   B. Lieutenant General
   C. Major General
3. **I was the first female director of?**
   A. Maintenance
   B. Communications
   C. Infantry

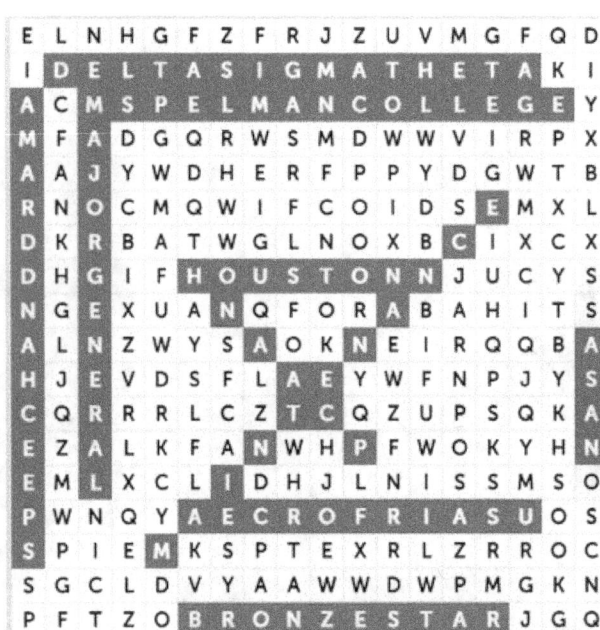

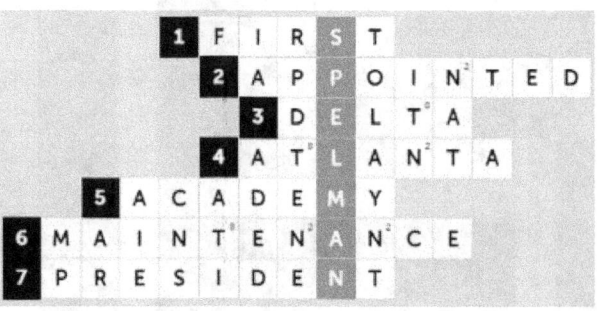

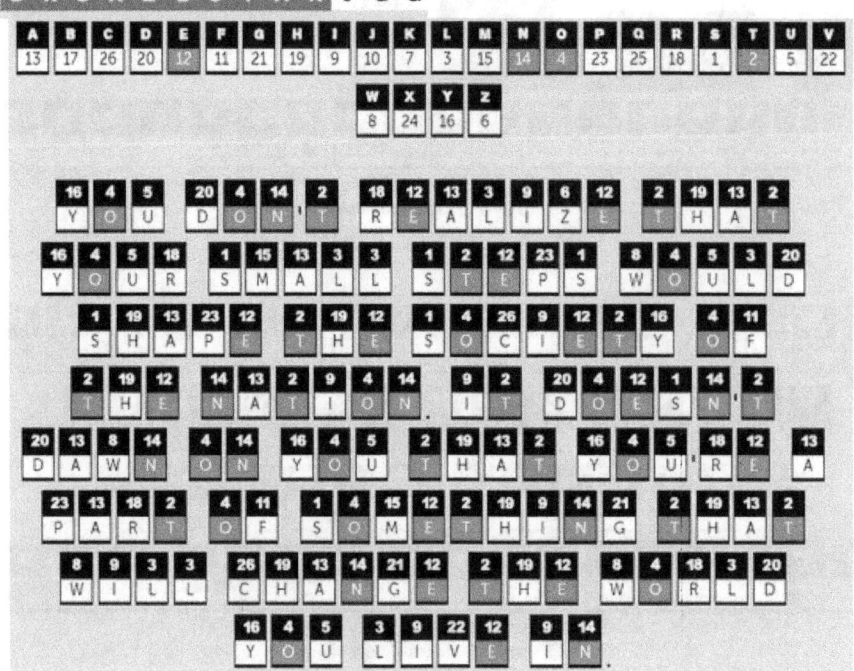

YOU DON'T REALIZE THAT
YOUR SMALL STEPS WOULD
SHAPE THE SOCIETY OF
THE NATION. IT DOESN'T
DAWN ON YOU THAT YOU'RE A
PART OF SOMETHING THAT
WILL CHANGE THE WORLD
YOU LIVE IN.

1. **What year did I become a second lieutenant?**
   A. 1936
   B. 1942
   C. 1954
2. **What aircraft didn't I fly?**
   A. P-39
   B. Curtiss P-40
   C. Curtiss P-36 Hawk
3. **I was the first African American to do what in the USAF?**
   A. Become an Officer
   B. Become a Brigadier General
   C. Become a four start General

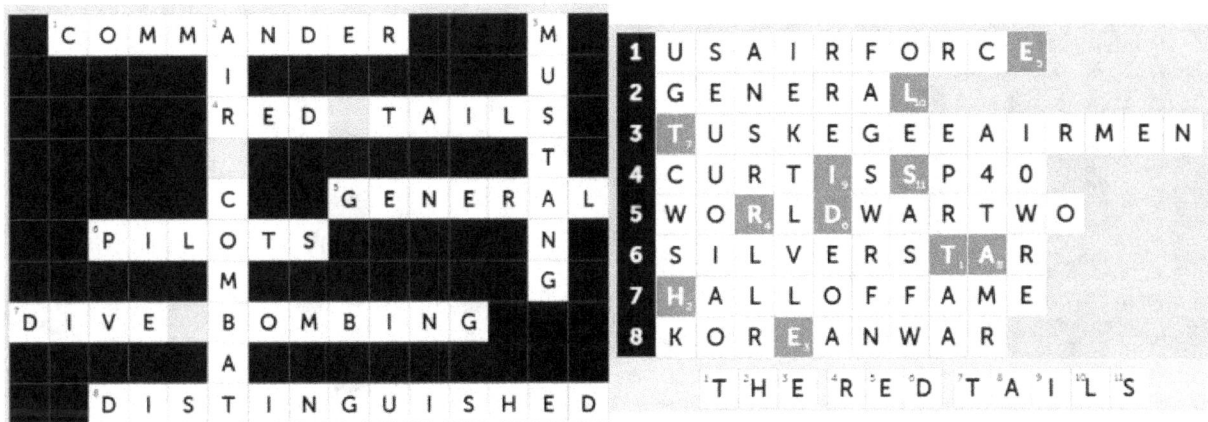

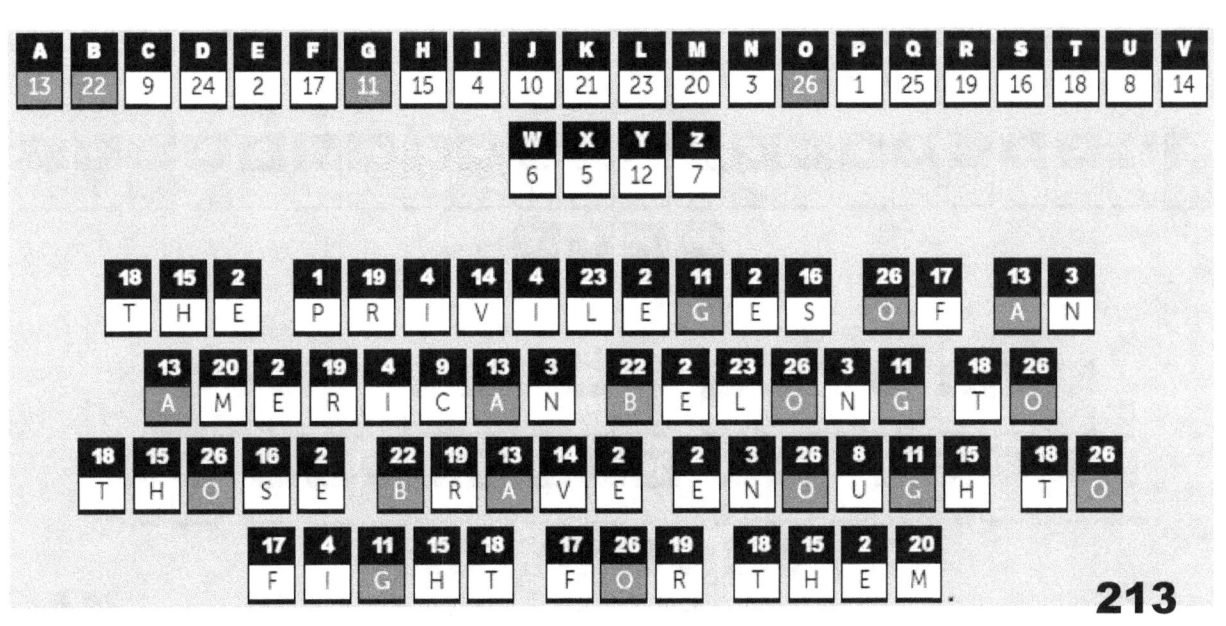

THE PRIVILEGES OF AN AMERICAN BELONG TO THOSE BRAVE ENOUGH TO FIGHT FOR THEM.

213

1. **What did I do in the Army before I enlisted?**
   A. Cook
   B. Nurse.
   C. Gunner
2. **What year did I enlist in the Army?**
   A. 1868
   B. 1865
   C. 1866
3. **I was the first black woman to do what?**
   A. Enlist in the US Navy
   B. Enlist in the US Army
   C. Enlist in the US Air Force

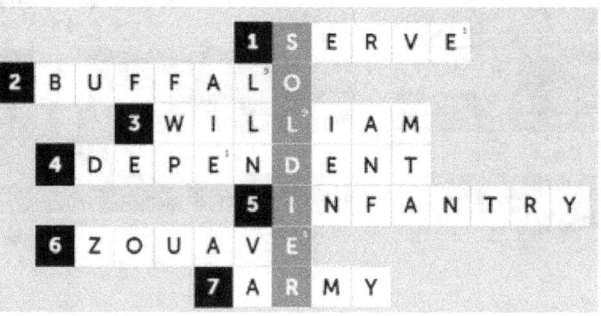

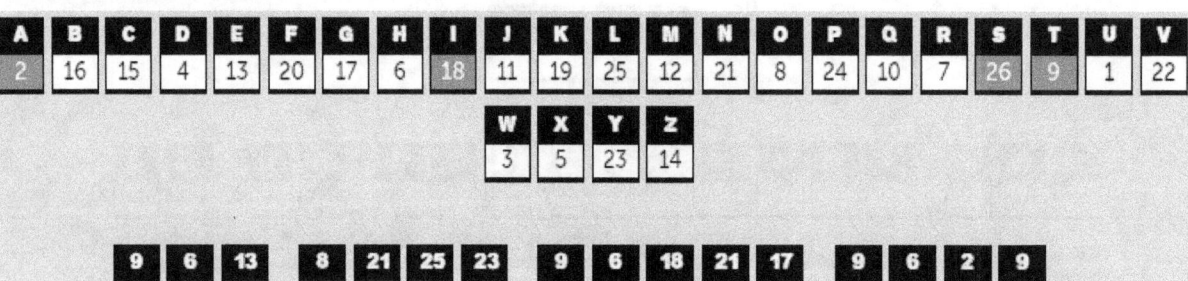

THE ONLY THING THAT RELIEVES PRESSURE IS PREPARATION.

1. **What college did I get my doctrine degree from?**
   A. University of Pennsylvania
   B. University of Toronto
   C. University of Virginia
2. **What year did I get my commission in the Army?**
   A. 1863
   B. 1865
   C. 1866
3. **I was the first African American to do what in the U.S.?**
   A. Hospital Administrator
   B. Join the Army
   C. Lead an Infantry Unit

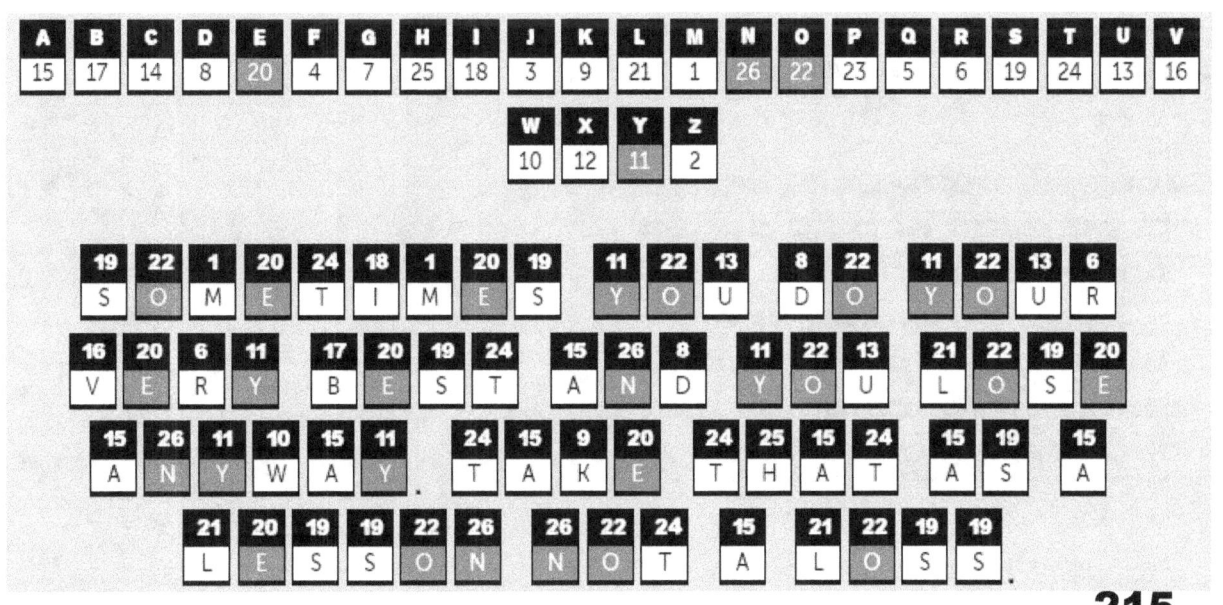

A	B	C	D	E	F	G	H	I	J	K	L	M	N	O	P	Q	R	S	T	U	V
15	17	14	8	20	4	7	25	18	3	9	21	1	26	22	23	5	6	19	24	13	16

W	X	Y	Z
10	12	11	2

SOMETIMES YOU DO YOUR
VERY BEST AND YOU LOSE
ANYWAY. TAKE THAT AS A
LESSON NOT A LOSS.

1. **What college did I get my Masters Degree from?**
   A. Smith College
   B. Columbia University
   C. Hunter College
2. **What was my rank in the Navy?**
   A. Lieutenant
   B. Ensign
   C. Major
3. **We was the first African American women to do what?**
   A. Become Enlisted in the Navy
   B. Recruit for the Navy
   C. Become Officers in the Navy

Harriet Pickens

1. **What was my Masters Degree in?**
   A. Medical
   B. Mathematics
   C. Social Work
2. **What college was I assigned to?**
   A. Smith College
   B. Columbia University
   C. Hunter College
3. **What did I work as, at the college?**
   A. Naval History
   B. Classification test administrator
   C. English

Frances Wills

Answers

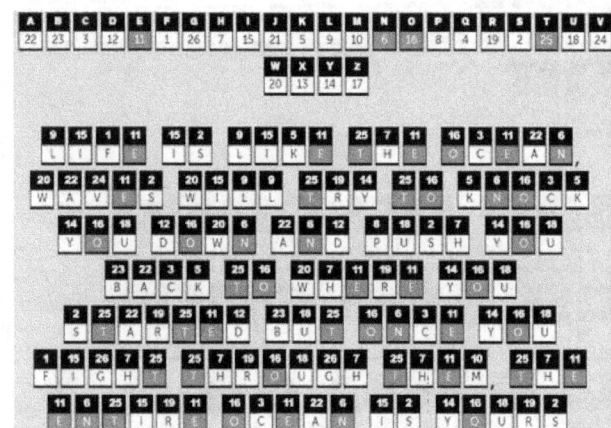

216

1. **What college did I get my Master Degree from?**
   A. Kansas University
   B. New York University
   C. George Washington University

2. **I became the first African American General in?**
   A. USMC
   B. USN
   C. USAF

3. **I was the first black Marine _____?**
   A. Grunt
   B. Technician
   C. Aviator

Frank Petersen

Answers

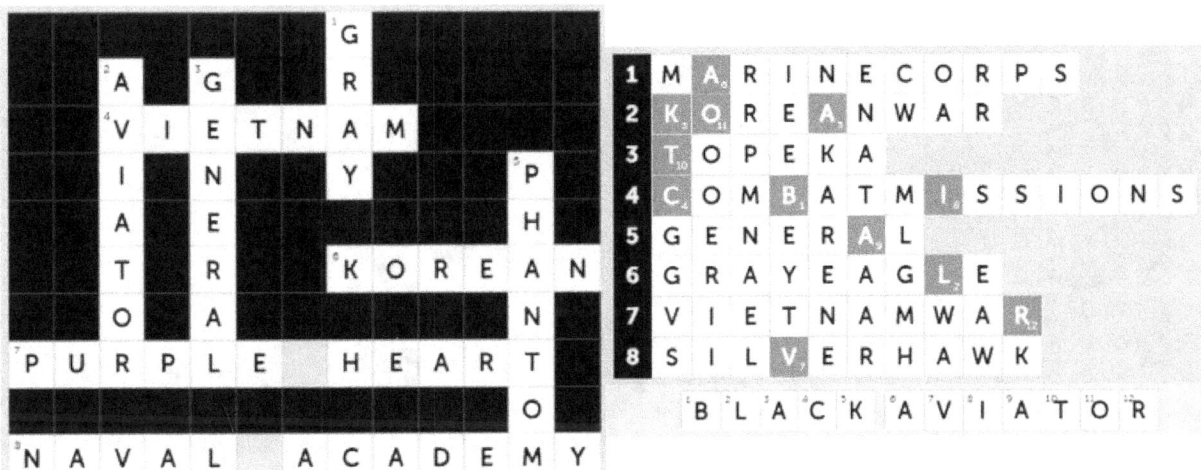

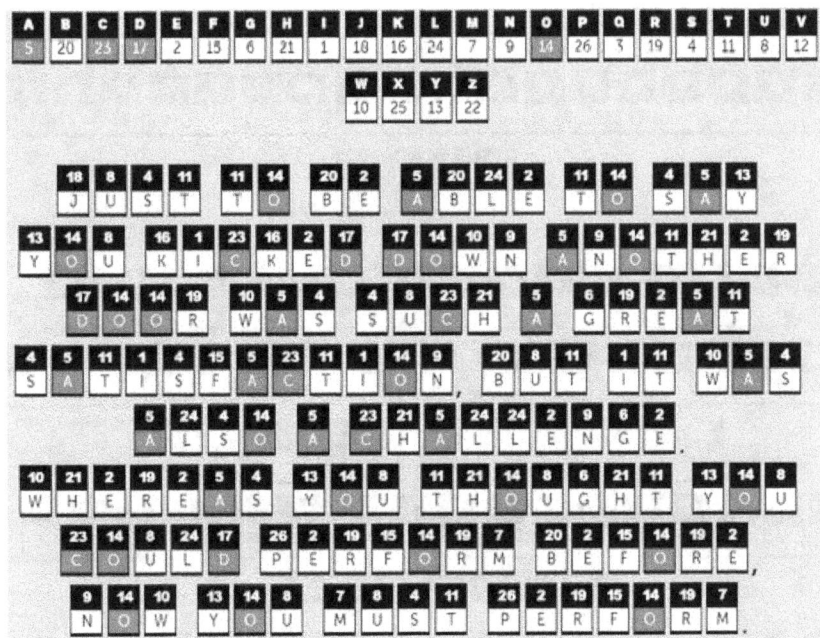

JUST TO BE ABLE TO SAY YOU KICKED DOWN ANOTHER DOOR WAS SUCH A GREAT SATISFACTION, BUT IT WAS ALSO A CHALLENGE. WHEREAS YOU THOUGHT YOU COULD PERFORM BEFORE, NOW YOU MUST PERFORM.

1. What college did I get my Bachelors Degree from?
   A. Kansas University
   B. University of Texas
   C. George Washington University
2. I became the first African American four-star General in?
   A. USMC
   B. USN
   C. USAF
3. Which regiment didn't I command?
   A. II Marine Expeditionary Force
   B. Marine Forces Europe
   C. U.S. 5th Fleet

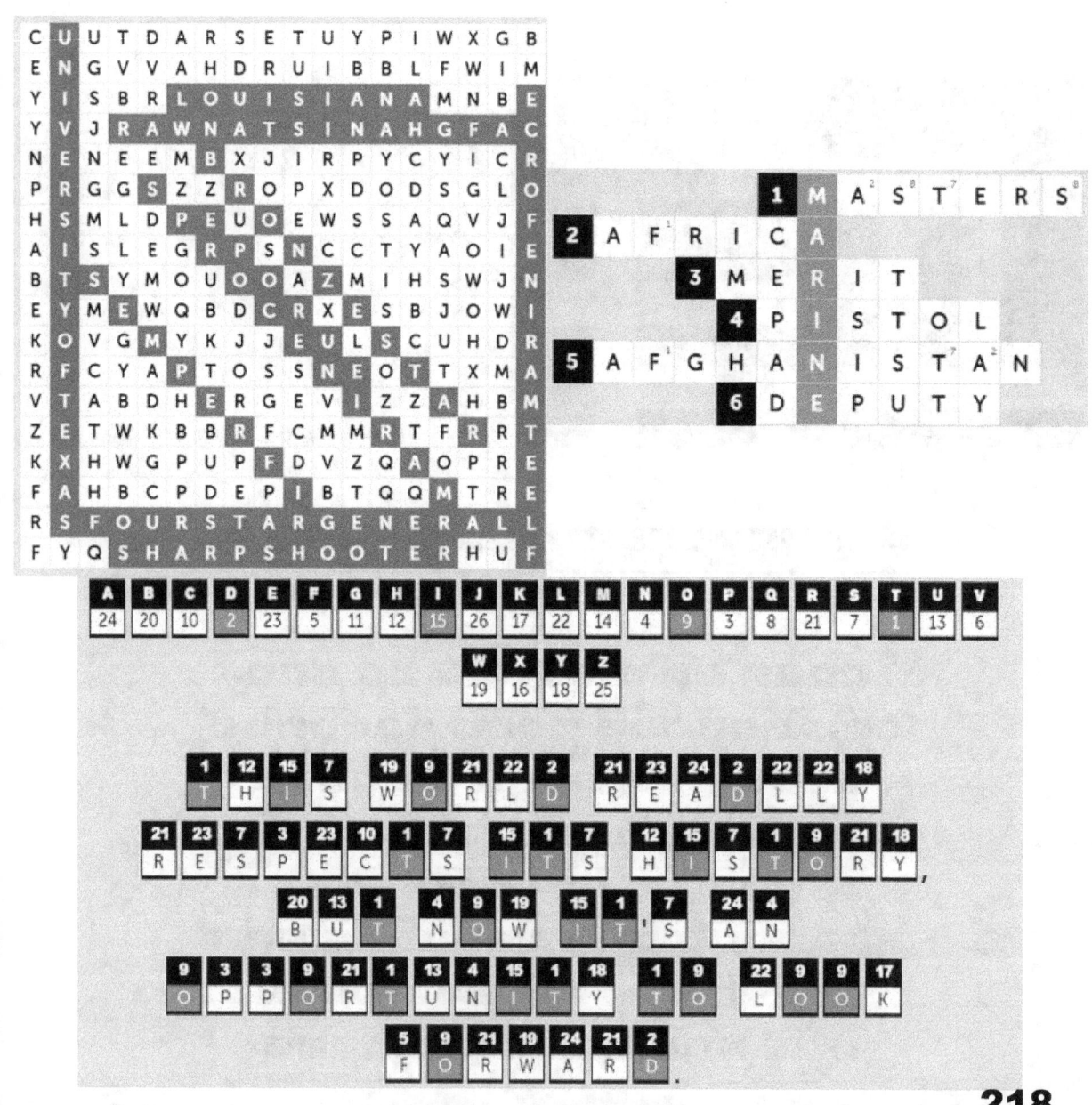

1. **What fraternity am I a member of?**
   A. **Omega Psi Phi**
   B. Alpha Phi Alpha
   C. **Phi Beta Sigma**
2. **What year did I did I get my commission with the USAF?**
   A. **1989**
   B. 1985
   C. **1983**
3. **I was the first African American to lead what?**
   A. A branch of the United States Armed Forces
   B. **A military University**
   C. **A military squadron**

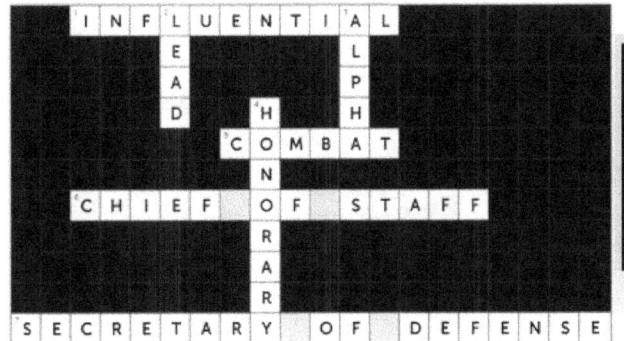

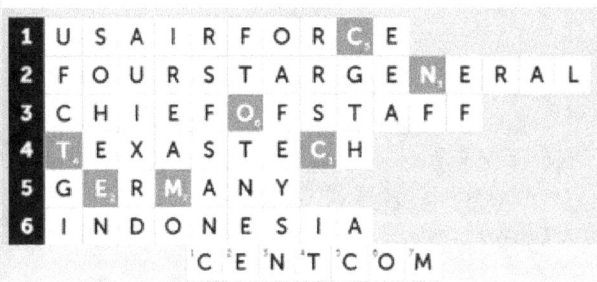

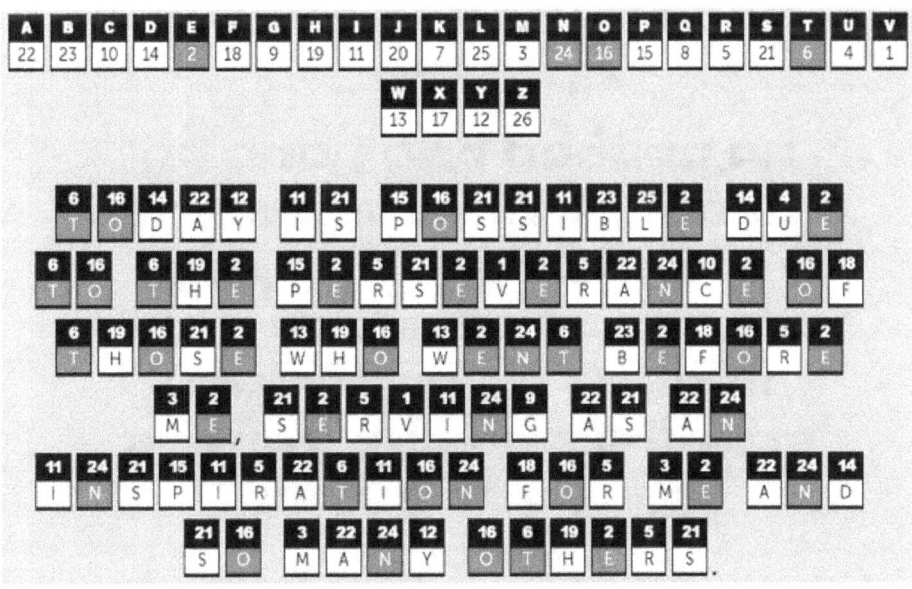

219

1. **What was the name of the ship I first took command of?**
   A. USS Hunley
   B. USS Rushmore
   C. USS Lexington
2. **What year did I become a four star admiral?**
   A. 2014
   B. 2012
   C. 2010
3. **I'm the highest-ranking woman in what branch?**
   A. United States Marine Corps history
   B. United States Army history
   C. United States Naval history

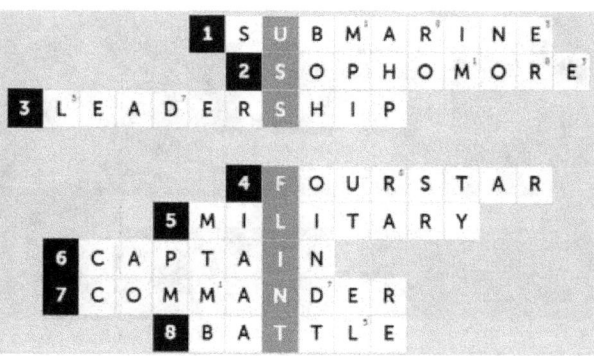

1. SUBMARINE
2. SOPHOMORE
3. LEADERSHIP
4. FOUR STAR
5. MILITARY
6. CAPTAIN
7. COMMANDER
8. BATTLE

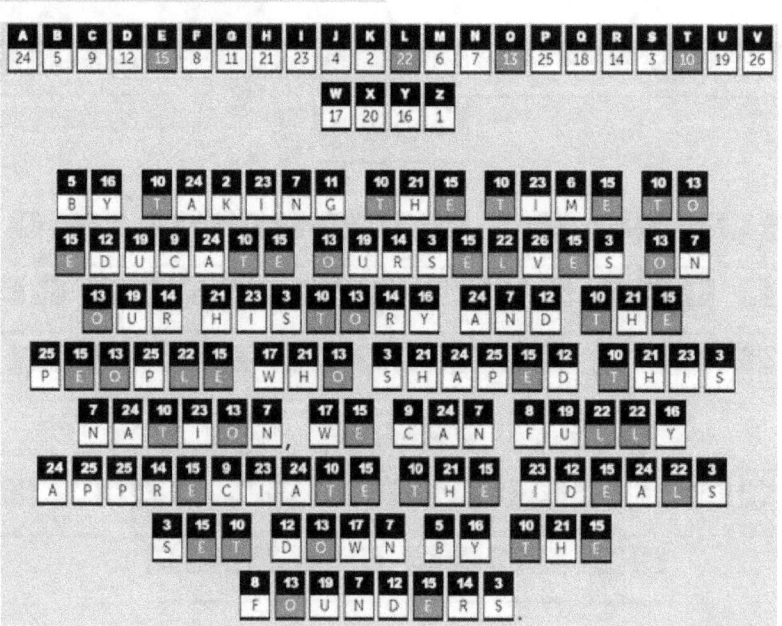

BY TAKING THE TIME TO EDUCATE OURSELVES ON OUR HISTORY AND THE PEOPLE WHO SHAPED THIS NATION, WE CAN FULLY APPRECIATE THE IDEALS SET DOWN BY THE FOUNDERS.

1. What was the name of the ship I was assigned to first?
   A. USS West Virginia
   B. USS Nevada
   C. USS Liscome Bay (CVE-56)
2. What year did Japanese aircraft carrier Akagi attack?
   A. 1939
   B. 1941
   C. 1943
3. I was the first African American to get awarded?
   A. Medal of Honor
   B. Purple Heart
   C. Navy Cross

Doris Miller

Answers

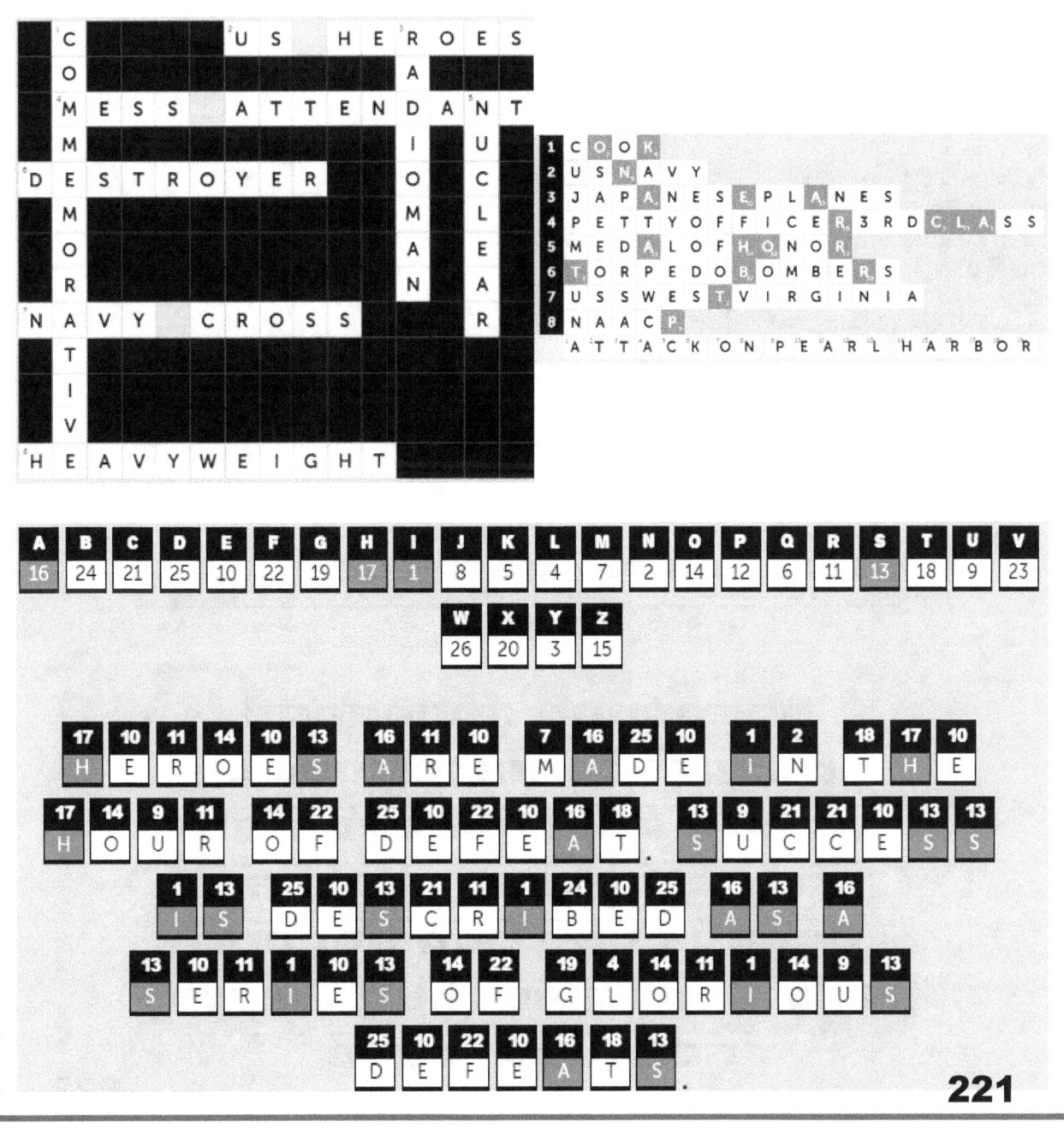

HEROES ARE MADE IN THE HOUR OF DEFEAT. SUCCESS IS DESCRIBED AS A SERIES OF GLORIOUS DEFEATS.

221

1. **What college did I get my Masters degree from?**
   A. Villanova University
   B. Catholic University of America
   C. Columbia University

2. **What year did I come back into the Army?**
   A. 1959
   B. 1955
   C. 1957

3. **In the Army I became the first black female to do what?**
   A. Become a head Nurse
   B. Become a General
   C. Become a Doctor

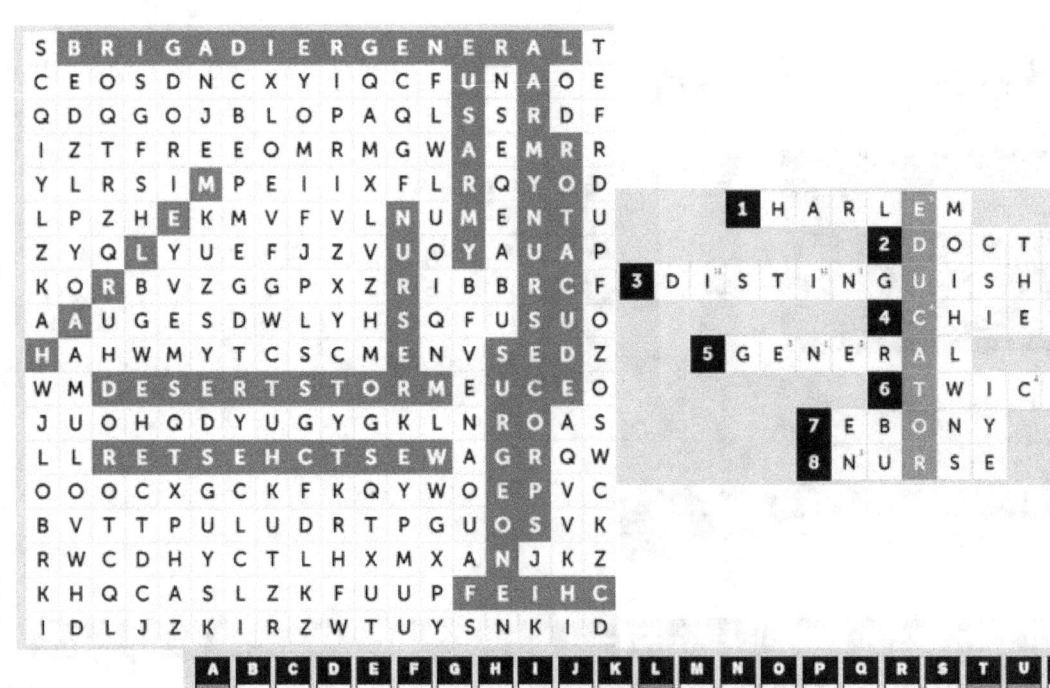

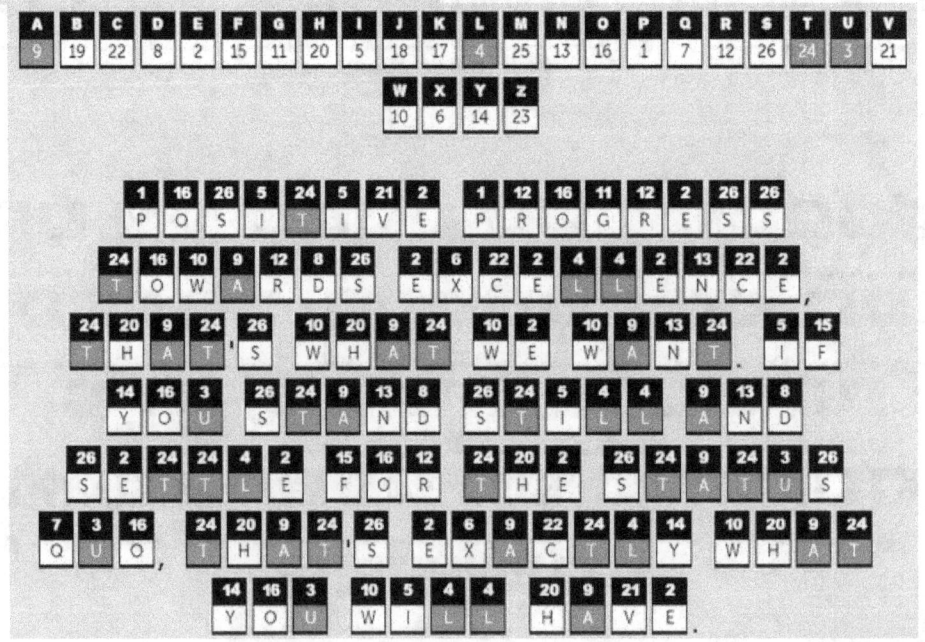

POSITIVE PROGRESS

TOWARDS EXCELLENCE,

THAT'S WHAT WE WANT. IF

YOU STAND STILL AND

SETTLE FOR THE STATUS

QUO, THAT'S EXACTLY WHAT

YOU WILL HAVE.

1. **What college did I go to?**
   A. Howard University
   B. Tuskegee University
   C. Fisk University
2. **What aircraft didn't I fly in the Korean War?**
   A. F-51 Mustang
   B. P-47 Thunderbolt
   C. F-80
3. **What year was I the highest ranking African-American?**
   A. 1975
   B. 1967
   C. 1970

Daniel James

Answers

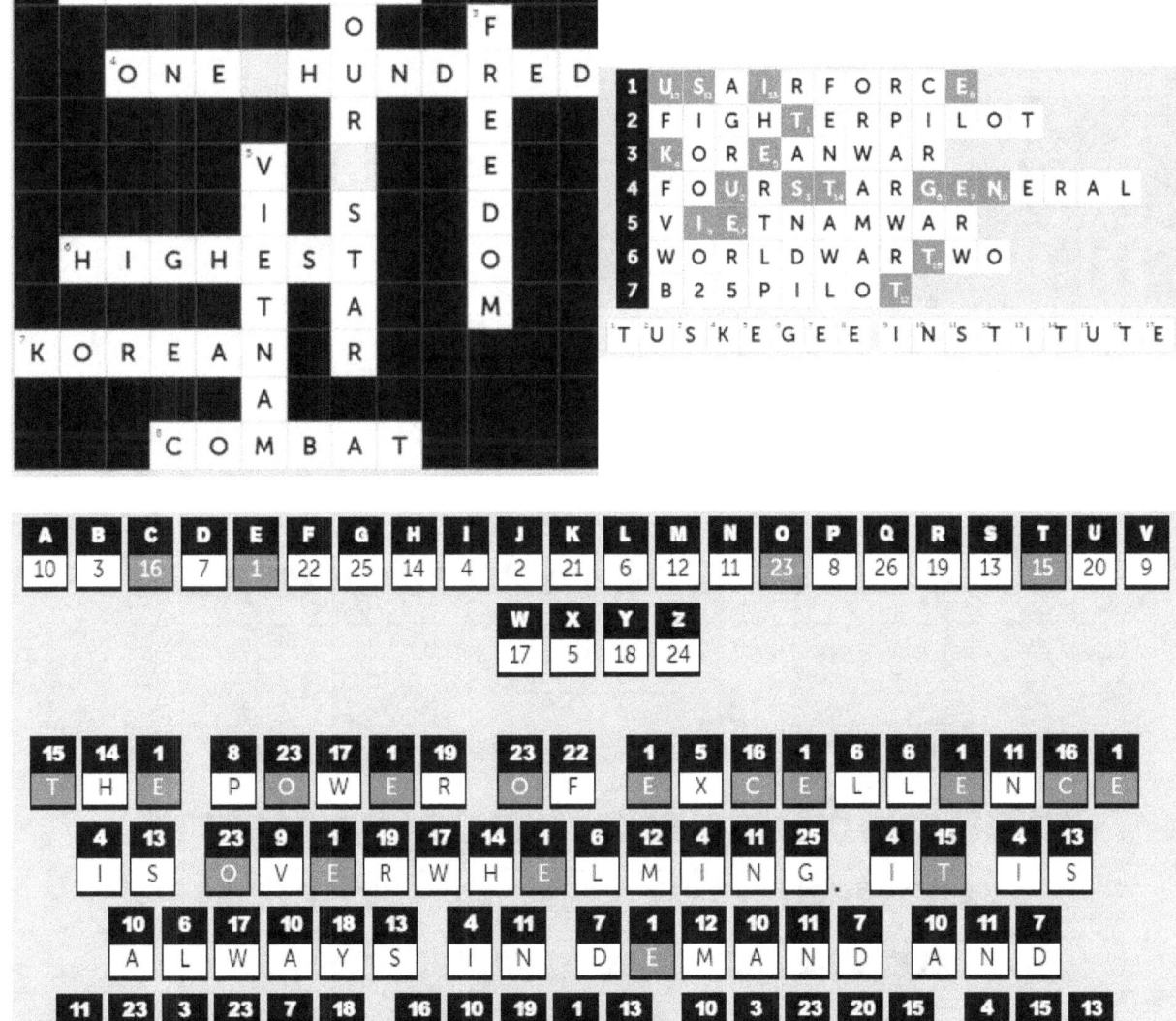

223

1. **What degree did I get from Springfield College?**
   A. **Masters**
   B. Bachelors
   C. **Ph.D**
2. **In 1948, President Truman issued what?**
   A. **Cease fire**
   B. Executive Order 9981
   C. **Mandatory Draft**
3. **I was one of the original?**
   A. **Temptations**
   B. Tuskegee Airmen
   C. **Super Soldiers**

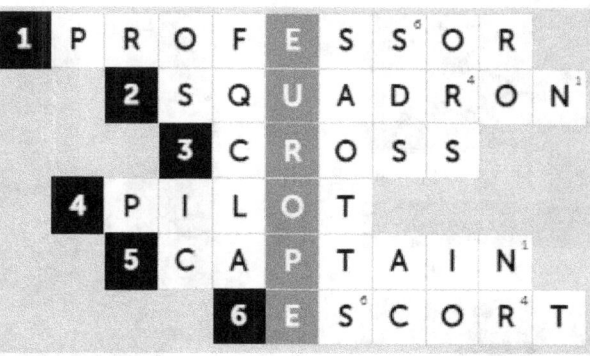

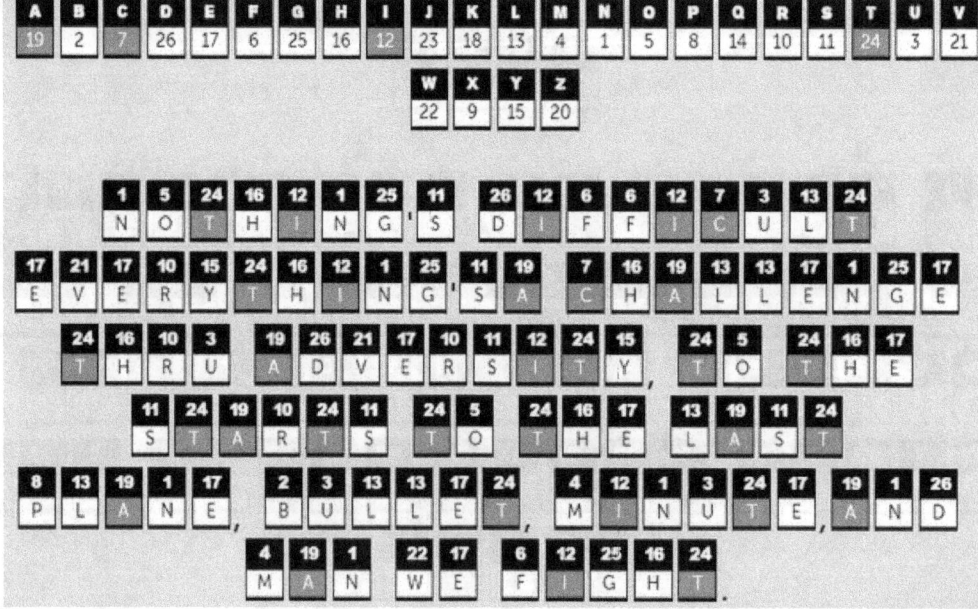

1. **What was the name of the college I went to?**
   A. Virginia Union University
   B. Hampton University
   C. Central State University
2. **What year did I get recalled to the Navy?**
   A. 1946
   B. 1949
   C. 1942
3. **I was the first African American to lead?**
   A. A Class room discusion
   B. A ship into combat
   C. A infantry unit into combat

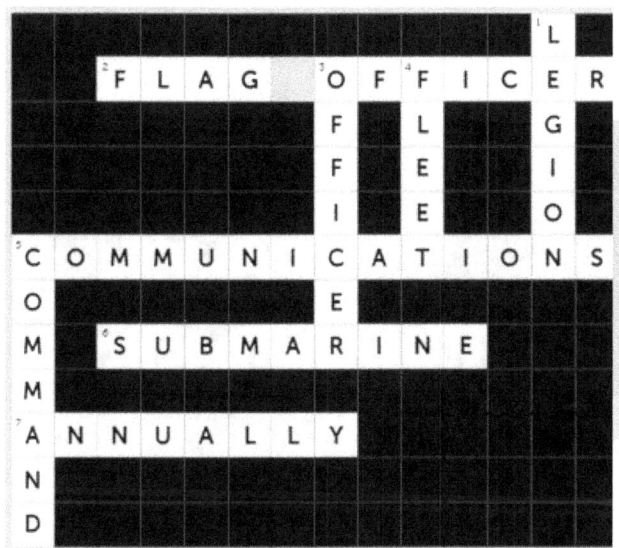

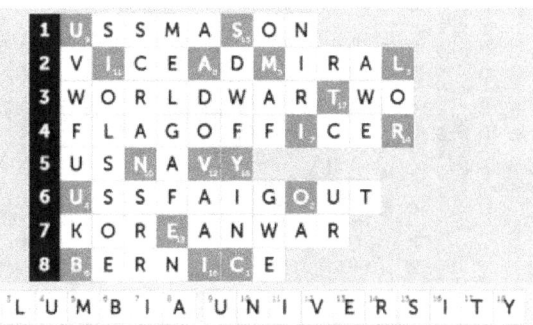

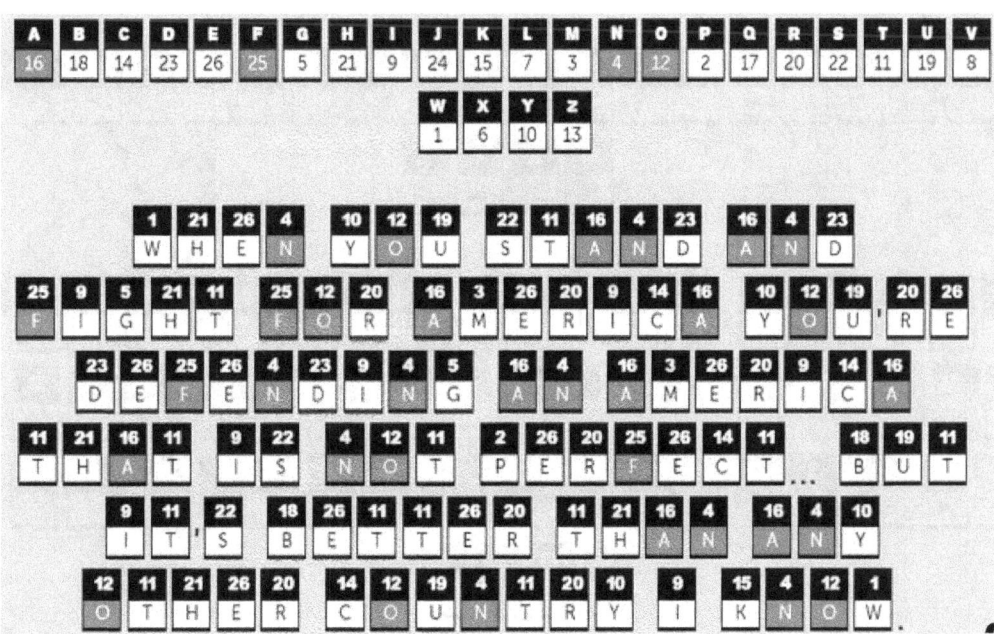

225

1. **What is the highest degree I have gotten?**
   A. Masters Degree
   B. Ph.D
   C. Bachelors Degree
2. **What year did I get my pilot wings?**
   A. 1960
   B. 1966
   C. 1963
3. **I was the first African American to do what?**
   A. Become an pilot
   B. Become an soldier
   C. Become an astronaut

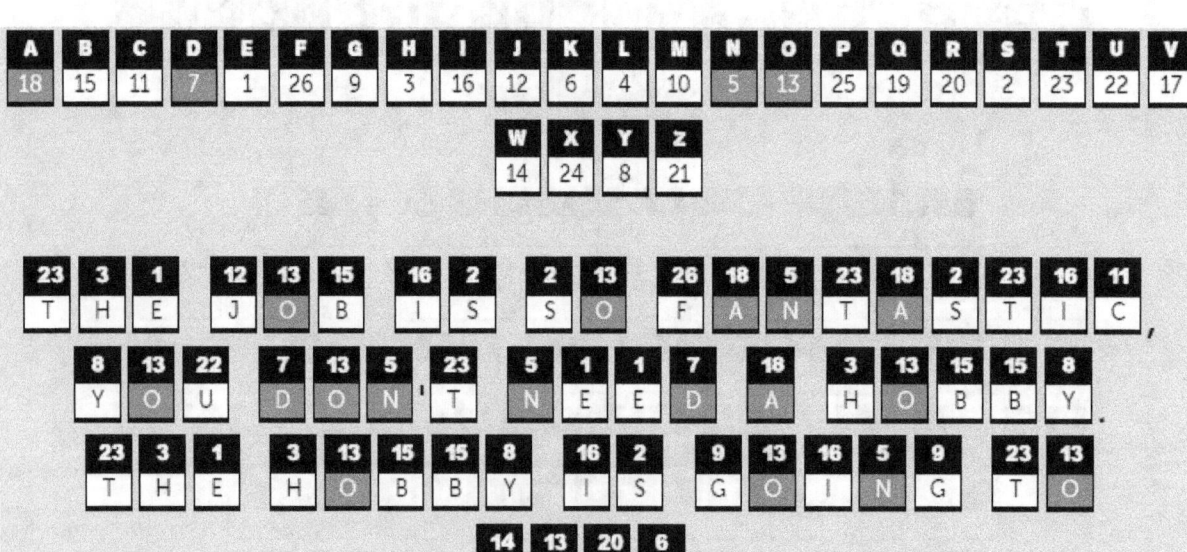

1. **What did I become when I joined the Army?**
   A. Tank Driver
   B. Mess Hall staff
   C. Paratrooper

2. **What war did I fight in?**
   A. Korean War
   B. World War II
   C. Vietnam War

3. **I was the first African-American to do what?**
   A. Get the Medal of Honor
   B. Get the Navy Cross
   C. Get the Purple Heart

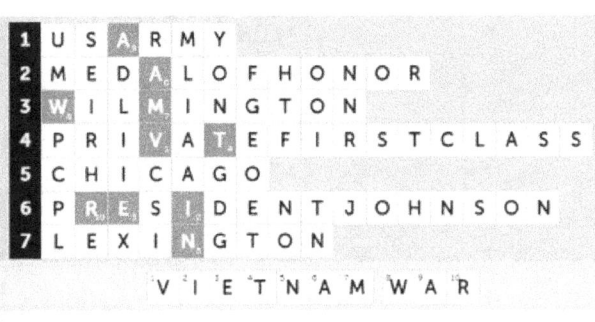

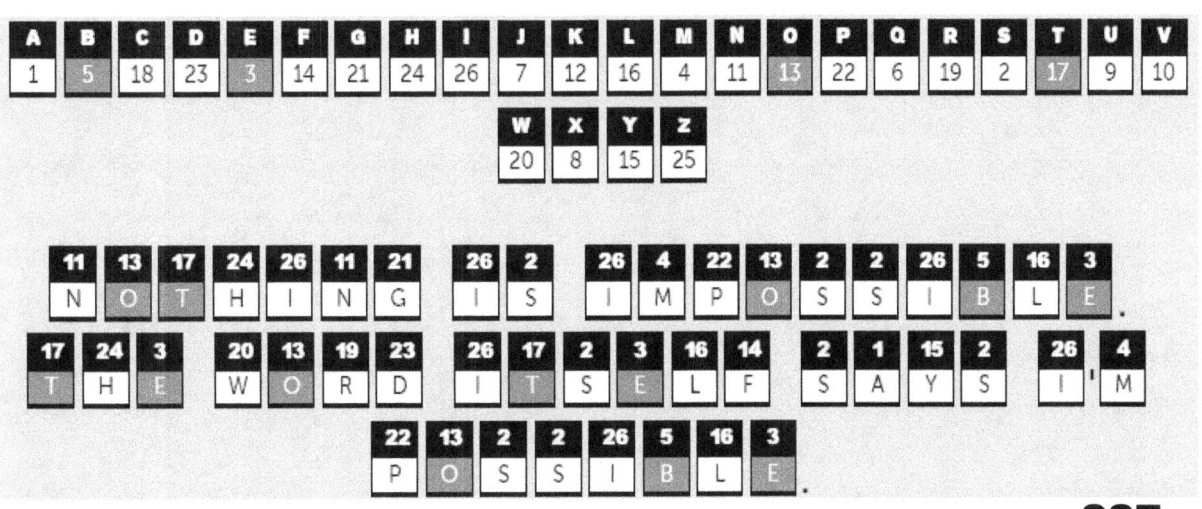

This book is dedicated to my grandkids
Anais Isabella Pablo-Antonio
Deyshawn Frank Chambers
Alicia Marie Jackson
Ayianna Marie Chambers
Zion Jamaris Jackson
Jayvon Jerome Jackson

ABOUT THE AUTHOR

Matthew D. Hale, the author of Black Historical Figures is a retired Marine and disabled veteran. He received his Bachelor of Arts in Computer Science from Campbell University and his Master of Science in Computer Engineering from Boston University. Matthew spends his down time making music, traveling, playing, and developing his own video games. Follow Matthew on Facebook/Meta at wegonnalearntoday, Instagram @ w_g_l_t and Tic Tok at wegonnalearntoday. Go to wegonnalearntoday.com or everydollarcountz.com for additional information.

In 2020 Matthew developed an interactive website, www.wegonnalearntoday, to provide access to Black History through games, music and videos. The website grew into the Black Historical Figures workbook series as a way to supplement the black history curricula taught in the school systems.

'In order to grow you must visit uncomfortable places'

10 BOOK SERIES
RELEASE DATES

NOVEMBER 2022

DECEMBER 2022

MAY 2023

AUGUST 2023

NOVEMBER 2023

GET YOUR COPY TODAY
DON'T FORGET TO TELL A FRIEND

www.ingramcontent.com/pod-product-compliance
Lightning Source LLC
Chambersburg PA
CBHW080727020726
47503CB00010B/2819